Lifted

HB S9

Hilary Freeman is an experienced journalist and agony aunt, working for national newspapers, magazines and websites, as well as on TV and radio. She has been agony aunt for *CosmoGirl!* and Sky and is currently a relationship adviser for askthesite.org. Her other jobs have included being a leg model and a very bad cleaner.

Hilary loves singing karaoke and doodling (her art teacher bought her school exam painting, but she hasn't sold anything since). Her first novel, *Loving Danny*, was shortlisted for the Lancashire Children's Book of the Year Award. She lives in Camden Town with her musician husband and the occasional pesky rodent.

Lifted

HILARY FREEMAN

PICCADILLY PRESS • LONDON

This book is dedicated to my friend Claire Fry
To new beginnings

First published in Great Britain in 2010
by Piccadilly Press Ltd,
5 Castle Road, London NW1 8PR
www.piccadillypress.co.uk

Text copyright © Hilary Freeman, 2010

A catalogue record for this book is available
from the British Library

ISBN: 978 1 84812 068 6 (paperback)

1 3 5 7 9 10 8 6 4 2

Printed in theUK by CPI Bookmarque Ltd, Croydon, CR0 4RD
Cover design by Simon Davis
Cover photo © Alamy

Mixed Sources
Product group from well-managed
forests and other controlled sources
www.fsc.org Cert no. TT-COC-002227
© 1996 Forest Stewardship Council
FSC

My Blog

This is a blog about shoplifting. And as it is my very first blog, the only thing I've ever written in the whole of the blogosphere, I'm going to come straight to the point. Yesterday, I stole something.

I was in one of those chain stores that sells everything, from underwear to cheap clothes to lamp shades, and the sort of knickknacks people buy for presents when they can't think of anything else: notebooks and picture frames and smelly bath oils. It's not a shop I'd usually go in, but I'd seen in a magazine that they were doing some vest tops in bright jewel colours for five quid a pair, and they were selling out fast, mainly because everyone who read that magazine (and who normally wouldn't be caught dead in that shop either) wanted them, which, of course, had made them even more popular. I know, I'm a sheep. Baa.

I took three of the vests into the changing room in my usual size: a red one, a green one and a purple one. The red one, which I tried first, was far too big, so I popped my head through the curtains to see if I could find an assistant to help me. There was no one about. Irritated, I got

1

dressed again and went back out on to the shop floor to find a smaller size. There were none on the rails, or in the pile on the shelves on top, except in a horrid salmon pink colour. Again, I looked around for someone to ask. Two female assistants were standing chatting by the Please Pay Here sign, totally oblivious to what was going on in the store. I put on my best pleading face, trying to catch their eyes but, if they noticed me, which I don't think they did, they chose to ignore me. Eventually, tutting loudly, I walked over to them and said, 'Excuse me, but have you got any more of those vests in an extra small?'

The taller assistant glowered at me, as if I'd rudely interrupted her private conversation. 'Dunno,' she said.

The shorter assistant, who had really bad skin, shrugged her shoulders. 'If there aren't any out, then we don't have any.'

'Could you check in the stock room for me, please?'

She tutted. 'Nah, they're all out.' And they went back to their conversation.

Now even more annoyed, I walked off without saying thank you. Not that they would have understood the words. I felt like announcing, 'Just so you know: I would have bought one in every colour (except salmon pink), if you could just have looked for me, or checked to see if another branch had them!' but what was the point? They didn't care about how many vest tops they sold, or whether a glossy magazine had written about the amazing quality of the cotton, any more than they'd care if I spontaneously combusted in the middle of the store, leaving bits of burnt flesh all over the cut price tea towels. They didn't care. Full stop. It made me so angry, irrationally angry. Angry and small. I can't explain why.

I walked away from them, intending to head straight for the exit, when something caught my eye. There was a pack of tights where it shouldn't have been, discarded next to a pile of T-shirts. Three pairs of extra-large, American tan tights, in a tea-coloured packet as ugly as its contents. American tan tights, the sweaty, nylon type that are supposed to be flesh coloured but don't match anybody's skin tone, not anyone in the whole wide world, whatever race they are. They don't even make fake tan that colour. Someone must have picked them up and then thought better of buying them, abandoning them to a lonely fate far away from the other tights. Unwanted tights in a store where nobody cared.

I don't know why, but I found myself picking up the tights and examining them, passing them from one hand to the other. Something inside me made me want to take them, even though I thought they were ugly and I knew they

3

wouldn't fit, and I'd never wear them, even if they did, not in a million, trillion years.

I couldn't see any security tags on them; they were almost begging to be stolen. I began to wonder what would happen if I took them. Would anyone notice? Would they care? Were there cameras in the store? Would an alarm sound as I went out? What would happen if I got caught? Would anybody understand that I really didn't want the tights? Would they ask me why I'd stolen them? My heart started beating very fast, my face flushed. Those tights were going to be mine, I was going to take them, I had to have them.

I picked up two T-shirts from the top of the pile and headed back into the changing room, pulling the curtain tight shut. I looked around me. The changing room was just a box, with three walls, a curtain and a bench. Nobody could see in and there weren't any cameras – they're illegal in changing rooms, aren't they? Then, breathing so fast I felt I might pass out, I opened up my bag and stuffed the box of tights deep inside. Taking in a gulp of air, I pushed my way out through the curtains, marched past the jewel-coloured vests, past the ignorant shop assistants and past the security barriers that framed the exit doors. As the doors parted for me, I held my breath and waited for a piercing siren, a hand on my shoulder, a shout . . . But there was only the noise of the traffic. I was out on the street again, and the hideous tights, the tights I didn't want but I had to possess, were mine.

Posted by Palgirl at 6:05 PM
Comments: 0
Followers: 0
Blog Archive
Links

Chapter 1

The boy watched the girl from his bedroom window, just as he had done many times before. She was sitting on the wall outside her house, apparently waiting for something to happen, or for someone to arrive. If she'd glanced upwards for a moment, she might have noticed him, and then he would have waved, but she didn't look up. Not once. She kept staring at the ground, as if she found her shoes fascinating. The boy supposed that she might have been following the progress of an ant or a worm along the cracks in the pavement. He screwed up his eyes and concentrated really hard, willing her to gaze up at him and smile. Then he imagined an invisible magnet attaching itself to the top of her head and gently pulling it towards him. But his powers of concentration could not have been strong enough, because her head did not move, not even a centimetre.

The boy's name was Noah, like the guy in the Bible who herded all the animals into the ark, two by two, and ended up on top of a mountain, while all the world drowned beneath him. Noah liked that story. He found it easy to picture himself floating in a big, empty world, with only binary creatures for company. Perhaps he'd fit better there. He was tall and stringy and gangly, uncomfortable with the length of his arms and prone to bumping into things. It wasn't his fault. He'd grown so quickly, his limbs expanding nightly like creeping vines, that he hadn't yet worked out how to control his body's new form. His eldest sister had rather unkindly nicknamed him Lurch, because he stooped, in the way that very tall people often do. She said it looked like his head was too heavy for him. 'It must be all those brains,' she teased, 'they must weigh a ton. And that *ridiculous* hair,' the dense, dark hair which covered his head like a carpet of soft bristles. 'That hair,' she said, 'and those long eyelashes, they're totally wasted on a boy.' Then she ruffled his hair with her fingers in a big sisterly way, like she always did, and Noah squirmed, like he always did, although secretly he quite liked it.

Noah wondered if the girl had noticed how much he'd grown. She always used to be taller than him, by a good head and shoulders, even though they were the same age, but it was an awfully long time since they'd stood back to back to compare heights. He remembered how she used to cheat by standing on tiptoes to make

7

herself taller, and how he'd pretend he hadn't noticed. Now, when he saw her from the window, or passed her in the street, she was always wearing heels, which amounted to the same thing.

The girl was named Ruby, because she was her parents' shining jewel, and because they liked an old band called The Rolling Stones, and she was born on a Tuesday. Noah only knew there was a song called 'Ruby Tuesday' because his mum had played it to him once. He didn't much care for The Rolling Stones; they all looked ancient, like bits of dried-up old leather. He didn't know what Ruby thought of The Rolling Stones now. Or anything else, for that matter. They hadn't spoken properly for about four years, not since secondary school had begun.

Noah and Ruby had been neighbours all their lives. Her house was situated at the other corner of their cul-de-sac, almost, but not quite, directly facing his. Noah thought a cul-de-sac sounded posh, but it wasn't really, it was just a street that didn't go anywhere. He supposed he was what people called the boy next door, except strictly speaking he was the boy opposite. If things had worked out like they did in the olden days, in stories, then they should have grown up and become sweethearts and, eventually, got married. But it wasn't the olden days, it was nowadays, and nobody is interested in the boy next door, or has a 'sweetheart', do they?

On the very first day of the very first term, he had called at Ruby's house as arranged and they had walked to the school gates together, chatting nervously. He had expected that they'd walk home together too but, by the end of that first day, Ruby had already found a new friend to walk home with. By the end of the week, she'd asked him to stop calling on her in the mornings and, by the end of that term, she'd stopped hanging out with him altogether. He had gone round after school one day to see if she wanted to go out on their bikes, just like he often did, and she'd said, 'No thanks, I don't want to do that any more.'

It had hurt him, deep in his gut, and for a while he'd wondered what he'd done wrong, but his mum said he shouldn't worry, he hadn't done anything, girls could just be like that sometimes. 'At this age they want to hang out with other girls and older boys, not boys the same age as them,' she'd said. She'd told Noah it was probably just a phase and Ruby would want to be his friend again someday, and that he should be patient.

Being patient wasn't a problem for Noah. He had some other friends, of course, and he had his computer, and he was pretty good with that – exceptional, some people said, like a mini Bill Gates. You needed to be patient while you waited for stuff to download or tried to crack a password. He'd got so caught up in his games and his codes and his software that he'd forgotten about Ruby altogether for a while, didn't really mind that she wasn't his friend any longer. He'd see her on the street, getting into the car with one of her parents, or leaning against the wall with some of her mates, and he'd nod at her as he walked past, in a neighbourly way, and get on with whatever he was doing. But, lately, for the past few months or so, he'd been feeling differently, and the fact that Ruby was no longer his friend had started bothering him again. He couldn't explain why, but whenever he saw her he felt a need to be close to her, to talk to her, and every time they passed each other without speaking, he felt what he could only describe as a twang of emptiness in his belly. And, he would never have told anybody this, but he had started having dreams about Ruby too – embarrassing dreams.

He looked down at her now and wondered if she ever thought about him at all, or remembered the times they'd spent playing together as little kids, bouncing a tennis ball against the garage doors. Maybe that was it, maybe she still saw him as a little kid. And maybe he was, at least compared to the boys she hung around with now, sixth formers with pecs and super-white trainers and rap on their MP3 players. His mum told him he was handsome, but mums always think that, don't they? All he knew was he didn't have the right clothes and he wasn't good at football, and the stupid thing was he didn't really care about those things anyway; it was just that *she* did.

He could see that she was on her phone, walking around in circles and moving her head and her arms about an awful lot, as if she was annoyed with whoever was on the other end. She was too far away for him to lip-read, and the sound of her voice didn't carry across the street, but he could now see that she had an overnight bag with her and so it didn't take a genius to work out that she must be waiting for her dad, and that he was late again, and she must be upset with him. Noah couldn't figure out why she didn't wait for him inside, but perhaps he didn't like to come into the house when her mum was there. Noah didn't know much about how divorced people behave; his parents were still together, and so were his aunts and his uncles and his parents' best friends. He knew he was lucky. Ruby's parents got divorced when she was twelve, by which time she was no longer speaking to him, so he didn't know how she felt about it. But he did know she really loved her dad and he had noticed that she didn't seem to smile as much as she did when they were kids, not when she was on her own, anyhow.

An email pinged into his inbox and he glanced down at his screen to read it. It was from one of his forum friends, a guy in Canada. Noah had contacts all over the world now, people who swapped software and tips with him. It was amazing how similar techie types were, he thought. Whether they came from Canada or Katmandu they all spoke the same language. It made him feel comfortable, like he belonged somewhere.

When he looked out of the window again, Ruby had

vanished. He hadn't heard a car pull up, and she hadn't had time to walk out of sight, so he guessed that she must have gone back inside her house. Maybe her dad wasn't coming today after all. He felt sad for her. Sad, and if he was honest, a tiny bit glad too, for himself, because it meant that she'd still be nearby.

He sighed and returned his gaze to his computer screen. He had a lot to do, emails to answer, some coursework, and then there was the project he was working on, the thing he was keeping to himself. Working on the computer made everything simple, if he let himself be absorbed by it. There were no surprises and no disappointments, only problems to be solved.

'Noah? Can I come in?'

The voice startled him. An hour or two must have passed; he had been concentrating so hard he hadn't been conscious of the time.

'It's OK, Mum,' he said.

His mum peered around the door, hesitantly, as if she wasn't sure what she might find inside. 'That was Pam from over the road on the phone,' she said. 'She wants to know if you can pop over there later.'

Noah felt his pulse quicken. Pam was Ruby's mum; he hadn't been invited into their house for years. He wondered if focusing hard on Ruby, willing her to look up at him, had in a strange way worked after all. He cleared his throat, so his voice wouldn't come out squeaky. 'What does she want?'

'Something about Ruby's computer being broken.'

Noah felt a pool of crimson spread across his ears and down his neck at the mention of her name. He hoped his mum hadn't noticed.

'Her dad was going to take a look at it, but he's stuck on some business trip. Mrs Taylor from down the road must have told them you're a bit of a whizz with a PC these days, and Pam wondered if you could fix it instead.' She smiled. 'Oh, and they said they'd give you twenty quid.'

Noah nodded. 'All right,' he said, trying to contain his excitement and his nerves. He didn't care about the money. 'I'll go round in a bit.'

He went over an hour later; he would have gone straight away, but he didn't want to seem too keen. Before he left, he changed his shirt and put on extra deodorant. He didn't think he smelled, not when he sniffed his armpits, but he'd heard you become immune to your own scent, and he didn't want to take the risk.

Pam let him in. 'Oh, hello Noah,' she said, in a faintly surprised tone, as if she hadn't been expecting him. He thought that was strange, given that she'd asked him to come. Maybe he was too early. Or maybe it was his appearance that startled her. He was conscious that people who hadn't seen him for a while often took in the length of his body, in the way they might have admired a tall building. 'Ruby's in her bedroom. I'll just get her for you. Ruby!' she called out. 'Noah from across the road is here! Can you come down please!'

Noah heard the padding of footsteps above him and Ruby appeared at the top of the stairs. She'd tied up her hair and changed since he'd seen her from the window. She looked so pretty close up, he almost gasped.

'Come up, Noah,' she said. She waited on the landing while he climbed towards her. Curiously, he noticed, his legs felt both as heavy as lead and uncontrollably light, at the same time. When he got to the top of the stairs she beckoned him to follow her. She must have forgotten that he knew where her room was; he'd been in it hundreds of times, just not for ages. Their houses were laid out exactly the same, except she had the room at the back, which, in his house, was shared by his two younger sisters. He had the box room, which, in Ruby's house, was used for storage. At least, it used to be. He followed her into her bedroom, trying to keep his pulse under control. He felt weird being there, alone with her, but she seemed oblivious. He wasn't sure what to do with himself, where to stand or sit, so he leant against the door frame, while she sat down on her bed. The room hadn't changed very much in four years. All the furniture was the same, and it was positioned the same, and the walls were still painted a sunny primrose yellow. There were far more blu-tacked posters now, of actors and singers and sports stars, and there was more make-up on the dressing table, and fewer toys, but that was to be expected. She was fifteen, not eleven.

'The computer's over there,' she said, pointing to her computer desk. 'Obviously.' She smiled, warmly. 'Do you need anything? A drink or something? I might be able to find some biccies.'

She was a still a kind person underneath, Noah thought, even though she wasn't his friend now. He shook his head.

The problem wasn't serious, it was just a matter of doing a basic rebuild of some of her files – something she could have done herself, if she'd known how. He was disappointed. He knew that if he told the truth and said, 'It's nothing,' and sorted it out in an instant, she'd thank him and then he'd just go home, and that would be that. He wanted to spend time with her – he realised he might not get another opportunity. So he said, 'Hmm, I can see what you've done. Don't worry, it's nothing too serious, but it's a job and it will take me a while to fix.' He hoped she hadn't noticed his shaky voice. He wasn't used to lying.

'Oh, right,' she said, getting up. She didn't seem interested. 'I'll leave you to it, then.'

'Well,' he began, and tried to think of a reason to make her stay. 'It's just that I might need you for passwords and stuff. It would be better if you were here.'

'Oh, OK then.' She shrugged and sat back down, hard, making the bed bounce. It reminded Noah of the times that they used to jump up and down on it, pretending it was a trampoline, until Pam told them off for wrecking the springs.

'It's been a while,' he said, smiling, hoping she'd remember too.

'It sure has,' she replied, in the vaguely amused tone people use when they're either not sure what you're talking about, or don't want to continue the conversation.

He fiddled around on her computer for a while, tidying her files and cleaning things up. He was still hoping she'd start chatting to him, but she didn't. She just sat in silence, thinking about something or nothing – he couldn't tell – although he was fairly sure she wasn't reminiscing about their shared childhood. He would have said something himself, if he'd known what to say, if he hadn't been so afraid of saying the wrong thing. Every so often, he'd glance around at her and smile in a goofy way, and she'd smile back, but only with her mouth. So he just got on with the job at hand. When he asked her for her passwords, he expected her to tell him to budge up, so she could type them in herself, privately, but she actually spelled each one out loud for him. She must have forgotten that he had a photographic memory; he would still remember them all weeks later.

'All done,' he said, eventually, twisting around in the chair. He couldn't think of any other delaying tactics. It wasn't as if she was talking to him anyway. Well, that's it, then, he thought, opportunity lost, and he made a move to get up.

'Before you go . . . ' she said, and, surprised, Noah sat back down. 'Do you know anything about blogs?'

'Sure,' he said, smiling to himself. There was nothing about blogs he didn't know. He'd been blogging even before they were called blogs. 'What do you want to know?'

She hesitated. 'It's not for me, I mean, it's not my blog, it's for a friend of mine. She wants to start one up and she's not sure the best place to look, or how to make it searchable and stuff.'

Noah wondered which friend she meant. There was the short girl with the blond hair and the shrill voice, the one who wore too much make-up – she might have been called Hannah, or Honey. And there was Amanda, the skinny one with black hair and shiny shoes, who all the boys seemed to like, although Noah couldn't understand why. 'It all depends,' he said, and checked himself. Ruby didn't need to hear a long list of technical specifications. That would be like announcing, 'Yes, you're absolutely right, I am a computer nerd!'

'Well,' he continued, 'there are some good ones, easy ones to use. I can set you – I mean, your friend – up if you want. Why don't you tell her to call me?' He took a deep breath, daring himself to say it. 'I could give you my number.'

'Yeah,' said Ruby. She paused again. 'Um, I'd rather you just showed me now, if that's OK. I mean, if it's not too much hassle.'

Noah was hurt. He figured that she probably didn't want her friend to find out that she knew him, or that they were neighbours. And she didn't want his number. She thought he was an embarrassment to her, didn't she? For an instant he felt like telling Ruby where to stick her friend's blog, but that feeling passed, and then he went back to feeling that he'd do anything for her, because when she was around he couldn't help himself. 'OK,' he said, getting up from the chair. 'You'd better sit down here and tell me exactly what your friend wants.'

Chapter 2

'But you promised!' said Ruby, stamping her foot on the pavement in frustration, even though the gesture was futile because the person on the other end of the phone couldn't see her do it, and she was wearing soft-soled sheepskin boots, which made virtually no sound at all. 'You said that you'd definitely be here today to pick me up, whatever happened! And you were going to look at my dodgy computer too.'

'I'm really sorry, Rubes,' said her dad for the third time, from wherever he was this time. Watford? Reading? Halfway down the M1? She hadn't taken in anything after 'I'm afraid I'm not going to make it today after all.' All that mattered was that he wasn't coming. 'Work is manic at the moment,' he continued, 'what with all the redundancies and cutbacks, and I really can't say no to the directors. It's not my fault the economic situation is so tough, now is it? It won't be like this forever.'

Ruby pouted, although her dad couldn't see this either. 'You always say that,' she moaned. 'It's always about money, or work, or whatever. What about me? Aren't I important too?'

'Of course you are. You're the most important thing in the world to me. Why do you think I work so hard? It's so I can look after you. I hate having to let you down like this, I really do.'

'You could at least have told me earlier, before I stood outside the house for an hour like a total idiot.'

'I did try, love, I tried several times, but you were on the phone all afternoon. I didn't just want to leave a message.'

It was true. She'd been talking to her friend Hanni for the best part of an hour, using up her free minutes, and then Amanda had called to tell her about the DVD she'd just seen, and . . .

'Still,' she said. 'It's not fair.'

'No, it's not. And I will one hundred and fifty per-cent be there next Saturday.'

'That's what you said last week,' she said. And, she thought, probably the week before, and the week before that. 'I don't believe you.'

'It really can't be helped, my love.' He sounded hurt, and she was glad. At least it showed that he cared. 'I promise I'll make it up to you,' he said. 'I'll think of something really special.'

Yes, she thought, he'd buy her something: some shoes or a designer bag or a stupid gadget, like he always did. She didn't want *things*, she wanted him to want to spend time with her.

'I'd better go – I'm on the hands free. I'll call you tonight and see you on Saturday, OK?'

'OK,' she said, sulkily. 'Bye, then.' She hung up the phone before he could tell her he loved her, or ask her to tell him the same. She wasn't in the mood, and anyway, it embarrassed her.

Now she'd have to go back into the house and unpack (what a waste of time choosing which clothes to take had been), and her mum would say it was such a shame that her dad wasn't coming, and she'd make that smug 'I'm disappointed for you but I can't say I'm altogether surprised' face that she always made when her ex-husband let Ruby down. And then Ruby would feel like she had to defend her dad because it really wasn't his fault, was it? She'd feel torn and confused and – what was that great word that she'd heard someone say? Dis-com-bob-u-lated, that was it. Yes, discombobulated, like someone had put all her insides in a giant mixing bowl and swirled them about.

When they'd split up, Ruby's parents had sat her down and made her a solemn promise: 'We'll never make you choose sides, Ruby. We'll never use you to

21

score points off each other and we won't bitch about each other to you. We love you equally and we want you to do the same.' It was what was called an 'amicable' divorce. There was no affair, no nastiness. They'd just fallen out of love, they told her, grown apart. Ruby knew that was supposed to make her feel better, but it didn't. She lay in bed at night wondering how, if two people really, truly loved each other, they could *just* fall out of love. It would almost have been better if something dreadful had happened to make them hate each other, so at least there was a tangible reason. Because if people could fall out of love for no reason at all, then it meant that nothing good lasted forever. What hope was there that she'd ever find anyone to love her eternally? And if her parents could just stop loving each other, who was to say that maybe, one day, they wouldn't just stop loving her too?

Noah was at the window again. Sometimes – and she might have been mistaken – she thought that he was watching her. Not in a creepy way – he wasn't a stalker, whatever Hanni had said, although she was ashamed to admit she had giggled at the idea – but in a sweet, protective way, like a fairy tale prince who yearns to save the princess imprisoned in the tower. Ruby laughed aloud at the notion of Noah as a prince (although not, it must be said, at the notion of herself as a princess). He was so lanky, so awkward, so overgrown. If he tried to clamber up a tower he'd be all arms and legs, like a chimpanzee. No, not a chimpanzee. That was too cruel, it made him sound ugly, which he wasn't. They'd been friends when they were little kids, but that was a long time ago, when she was another person. She'd read somewhere that every seven years all the cells in your body change entirely: they undergo a complete turnover. She didn't know if it was true, but it was a good notion. It must have been almost five years since she and Noah had been proper friends, so by now, nearly all her cells would have turned over – her hair, her skin, even the ones in her brain. She really wasn't the same person. Maybe that was why when she looked at pictures of herself when she was little, at that sweet, wide-eyed girl with dimples, it felt like she was looking at a distant cousin, at someone with similar features, who she knew only vaguely.

She couldn't remember exactly how it had happened, how she and Noah had gone from being best friends to being nothing, but she knew they had drifted apart around the time that her parents were arguing a lot. She hadn't wanted to spend time with anyone who knew her too well, then. It was easier to be around strangers, people who didn't know what was going on at home, people who wouldn't ask questions, or give her sympathetic looks. That way, she could pretend everything was normal. And by the time everything was normal again – the new normal, after Dad had left – she had a big group of mates, and Noah just didn't fit. Not that he'd want to. He was a superbrain, interested in completely different things. He didn't look like one of the nerds, but he'd ended up among them. People like him made her feel stupid. If they tried to make conversation with her, she'd become self-conscious and anxious that she didn't have anything interesting to say. She didn't mean to be rude, or abrupt, it just came out that way. Everyone – her parents, the teachers – said she was bright, and she got decent marks (deliberately not so high as to make her stand out, of course), but she felt like a fraud. So she reasoned that if she just said a brief hello to Noah when they passed, and walked on, she wouldn't get found out. It wasn't as if she missed him; she had plenty of friends, she didn't need one who lived across the street.

'Hi Mum,' she called out as brightly as she could, as she let herself back into the house. 'I'm home!' She tried to made it sound like she wasn't bothered about her dad not turning up, as if she'd intended to stand outside the front door for the best part of an hour for no good reason.

Her mother came into the hall. She gave Ruby *that* look and sighed, but didn't say anything. Ruby was thankful. 'I'll just dump my bag upstairs,' she said, her foot already on the bottom step.

'OK, love, I'll put the kettle on. And we can have those cookies I made too, the chocolate chip ones.'

Mum was always cooking for other people. She'd

prepare hearty casseroles for sick friends and bake cakes coated in buttercream to sell at charity fairs. For gifts, she enjoyed filling up boxes of the finest Belgian chocolates with hand-picked selections. 'There's nothing that can't be solved with chocolate,' she always said. Except obesity, Ruby thought. It was funny how both her parents believed that giving her things – food, clothes, jewellery, cash – would make her happy, when it was obvious to her that they would only make her spoiled and fat, if not perfectly accessorised. Her parents were pretty stupid for grown-ups.

When she came down the stairs, there was a mug of tea and a plate piled high with crumbly cookies waiting for her on the kitchen table. She sat down and cupped her hands around the mug until it grew too hot to touch, and her palms felt wet with condensation. The cookies looked and smelled good, but she wasn't hungry, so she played with a renegade chocolate chip, pushing it around her plate until some of the chocolate melted under her fingernail. She scraped it out with her tooth. It probably wasn't very hygienic, but it tasted good.

Her mum was on the phone. 'They can't do anything without them these days,' Ruby heard her say. And then, 'Thank you. That would be wonderful. We'll pay, of course. Would twenty pounds be all right? Lovely. We'll see him later, then.' She put the phone back on to the receiver and turned to Ruby, looking pleased with herself. 'I've found someone else to look at your PC, love. Noah from across the road. Apparently, he's good with computers.'

'Oh,' said Ruby, a little sharp with surprise. 'OK. I mean, thanks Mum.' Of course he was good with computers. Noah had been good with computers when they were seven. Truth be told, he was probably better with computers when they were seven than she was now. She could just about manage to switch hers on. After that, if it wasn't something as basic as sending a message or downloading a track, she was clueless. The way things worked, their insides, didn't interest her. She left that stuff to people like Noah. She didn't mind him coming round, she decided, as long as she didn't have to talk to him, because that would be awkward and tedious. Better to think of him as any PC repair man, a stranger, which he practically was now, anyway. She'd be polite, then leave him alone to get on with the job.

In the event, he came round much sooner than she'd anticipated, but that was good, it meant that afterwards, she could still do something with the day. She was amused to notice that he bounded after her up the stairs, like an overgrown puppy. He seemed so nervous and so excited to be at her house again. It was quite sweet, really, if not a touch pathetic.

Maybe Hanni was right about him. Maybe he had developed a big crush on her. That's probably why he wanted her to stick around while he worked, when he could just have asked her to write her passwords down for him. She didn't want him getting any ideas about them becoming friends again, or anything else, for that matter, and she wondered if it would be kinder to set him straight there and then. 'Look, Noah,' she could say. 'You're very nice and all, and I know we used to be friends way back, but don't get the wrong idea, OK? You and me? I don't know what's going on in your head, but it's never going to happen. And I've got a boyfriend, all right?'

She thought about saying it, but she concluded that she didn't want to be cruel. Why hurt him for no reason? Liking her wasn't a crime. And what if she was wrong and he wasn't interested in her at all like *that*, but just being friendly? As for that last bit, about the boyfriend, it wasn't even entirely true. There was Ross, from the year above, who snogged her from time to time and tried to cop a feel at a party, but he never took her anywhere on her own, or called her, or even talked to her much. She suspected that he used her like a fashion accessory. He'd say things like, 'We look good together, hon, don't you think?' And she had to admit that they did.

In a way, it was good that Noah made her stay in the room while he worked on her computer, because it meant she could ask him about blogging. A group of them had been talking at school about starting up blogs, but none of them knew anything about the technical side, how to go about it, or where to start.

'The thing about blogs is that you can write whatever you like,' Hanni had said, 'and no one has to know it's you. Unless you want people to, that is.'

Ruby had laughed at that. She knew there was no way on earth that Hanni could ever write an anonymous blog because she liked being the centre of attention too much. She'd want to be one of those bloggers whom everybody talked about and whose blogs were turned into a juicy book, which became a bestseller. But that was never going to happen, because writing a blog evidently involved *writing*, and Hanni hated writing anything. Texts were OK, as they were short, and emails too, because you could get away with text speak in them, but writing anything longer than a paragraph was torture for Hanni. Ruby usually did her English assignments for her, in return for music downloads and makeovers.

Amanda was different. She liked writing. And she was funny too. She said she might like to write a blog about the teachers at their school and what was really going on in the staff room, but that would absolutely have to be anonymous, or she'd get expelled. Or sued. Or both. She wanted to write a blog that would shock people. Casey said she was planning to blog about boys, while Debs said she couldn't think of anything to write about. Ruby didn't say very much at all. She had a few ideas, but nothing she wanted to share with the others. The discussion ended with everyone pledging to start their blog the very next weekend, but, as far as Ruby knew, nobody had done anything about it.

Noah showed her how easy it was to set up a blog. You just had to choose the type you wanted and sign up to it. It was so easy that she felt embarrassed for asking. See, that's why she didn't talk to him these days. He made her feel stupid and ignorant and girly. She decided there and then that she wouldn't tell the others that Noah had helped her. She'd show them all how to create their own blogs and say she'd worked it out for herself.

After Noah had gone home, she rang Amanda. She didn't want the day to be a complete waste. 'So, do you wanna go shopping?' she asked, without introducing herself. There was no need. They spoke so often that every new call felt like an extension of a previous conversation, albeit one with a long pause in between sentences.

'Hey you, I thought you were with your dad.'

'Long story,' Ruby said, flatly. 'Actually, short story. Too boring to explain. But I'm not. So, do you want to?'

'Sure, why not? I could do with some new jeans. What do you want to get?'

'I have no clue,' Ruby said. 'The sales are on and I just feel like shopping. You know.'

Of course Amanda knew. She was a girl, wasn't she? She understood that you don't go shopping because you need something. Well, of course you do, sometimes, but that's not the only reason, and definitely not the main reason. Going shopping isn't about *having* things, it isn't about *owning* them, it's about *acquiring* them. Because however amazing what you buy seems in the shop, however much you just have to have it because it's perfect and it makes you look three sizes smaller, and it goes with your eyes, by the time you get it home it's just another dress, or another top. Just a thing, like all the other things you already possess. It was, Ruby thought, a bit like being Cinderella at midnight. She wondered exactly when it was that the shopping spell was broken. Did it happen, imperceptibly, as she walked out of the shop or somewhere on the way home? Sometimes she bought things and took them right back the very next day, without even taking them out of the bag, or unwrapping the tissue paper. And sometimes, if she couldn't find the receipt, or if she left it too long, she would stuff the unwanted item to the back of the wardrobe, tags still attached, where it would remain, undiscovered, for months.

'I get it,' said Amanda. 'I'll meet you on the high street in half an hour.'

My Blog

January 21

I still don't know why I took those tights. Maybe I'll never know. All I can say is, oh my God, for a few minutes at least, it made me feel incredible, amazing, the way it must feel to win the lottery or sign a record deal. It was as if I was invincible, eight feet tall, like a supermodel or an A-list star at a premiere. I floated down the high street on a magic carpet of adrenalin, my body seemingly weightless, boneless and jointless. I didn't even need to breathe. It was a supercharged version of the buzz you get when you buy something you really, really want, only a million times more intense and a billion times more thrilling.

I suppose this is the part where I should say, don't try this at home, folks, because it's dangerous and stupid and against the law. So I'll say it now: don't try this at home. Stealing is wrong, it's a crime, it's a sin. Everyone knows that. Commandment number whatever: Thou shalt not steal.

Anyway, I don't know if this makes it better, or worse, but the buzz didn't last very long. Even less time than it does when you buy something, if I'm honest. It was gone before I'd turned into my road, and by the time I had walked through my front door I felt a little sick, a bit empty, like something was missing inside me, but I couldn't say what.

31

I took a peek at the tights in my bag, the horrible, ugly tights, and I felt foolish for taking them. Foolish and pathetic. It wasn't worth the risk, not for those tights. What had I been thinking? Mum noticed I was quiet and asked me what was up.

'Nothing,' I said. 'I'm just tired.'

And I was tired, so exhausted that it was as if all the adrenalin in my system had drained out of me. Still, I couldn't sleep. I turned and I tossed, wanting to talk to someone, to confess what I'd done, but knowing I couldn't. Who would understand, anyway? I managed a few hours and woke the next morning with what you might call a shoplifting hangover, a dull ache of guilt and a sickly feeling in the pit of my stomach. When I opened my eyes the very first thing I thought about was the packet of tights in my bag. It was as if they were calling to me from across the room, 'We're in here, you can't forget about us, we won't let you forget about us.' I tried to ignore them but they kept calling me. 'Look at us! We're he-ere! Let us out!' I put my bag inside the wardrobe and shut the door tight, but I could still hear them. Even when I went downstairs and ate my breakfast at the kitchen table, I was aware of their muffled voices in the distance. 'Shut up,' I whispered. 'Go away, leave me alone.'

If one thing was clear, it was this: I had to get rid of those tights. It wasn't because I was worried about anyone finding them, or because I needed to destroy the evidence, or anything like that. I just didn't want to have them in my possession for another moment. I toyed with the idea of taking them back to the shop and leaving them where I'd found them, but that was too risky. What if I got caught putting them back? It would have been easy to hide them in the dustbin, or, if I'd wanted to be ultra cautious, I suppose I could have walked up the street and thrown them away in a litter bin or a skip. But chucking them away didn't feel like the right thing to do. Whatever I did with them had to mean something. Otherwise, I would be not only a thief, and a stupid one at that, but a waster too.

It took me a few hours to figure it out. I was waiting at the bus stop when I saw an old lady struggle off a bus with her trolley and about eight plastic bags. As she stepped on to the pavement one of the bags caught in her skirt, revealing her swollen legs. She was wearing tan tights with holes in. At once, I realised what I had to do. No, not give her my tights, although I was tempted for a second. Imagine what she'd have thought if I'd run after her waving a packet of spare tights, like some sort of superhero . . . Hosiery Girl to the rescue! No, seeing her made me think there was bound to be someone, somewhere, who needed a pair of American tan tights, maybe somebody who couldn't afford to buy them. It struck me that I could do everybody a favour by giving my tights to a shop that did care – to a charity shop.

Maybe it would even cancel out the fact I'd stolen them.

There are about eight different charity shops in my area, so I had plenty of choice. But how do you decide between cancer and mental illness or homelessness and sick animals? Draw straws? In the end, I plumped for the one with the prettiest windows, the one where they'd made the most effort. The cancer shop had a colourful display with tinsel and paper flowers and mannequins wearing dresses that were almost trendy. Somebody had tried really hard to make it look inviting.

I took a deep breath and pushed open the door. The shop smelled fusty, like a damp garage. 'Hello dear,' said the woman behind the counter. She had grey hair and kind eyes and could have been aged anywhere between forty-five and seventy; I really couldn't tell.

I walked up to her and cleared my throat. 'Uh, hi. Um, I have something for you,' I said. I realised I'd never given anything to a charity shop before and wasn't sure how to do it. Did they even take things like tights? Would it be obvious mine were stolen? Too late now. I reached into my bag and pulled out the tights. 'I found these in a drawer,' I continued, inventing a story on the spot. 'They were my gran's. She died recently.' I crossed my fingers while I said it, to protect my both my grans, who are still very much alive. 'We were clearing stuff out. I mean, obviously I don't want them, but I thought you could sell them to someone. For charity.'

'Thank you,' said the volunteer, who didn't appear to notice that I was babbling nervously. She took the tights from me. 'That's very kind of you.'

'I know they're not much, but they haven't been worn and I will bring some other stuff in too soon. Good stuff, that is.'

'We're very grateful for any donations,' said the woman, smiling gently. She examined the packet, noting that the seal was unbroken. 'You'll be surprised how well unworn hosiery sells.'

I watched her as she peeled off a tiny white sticker from a sheet and stuck it to the top left-hand corner of the box. She paused for a second, chewing her pen thoughtfully, and wrote '20p' in neat handwriting. I beamed. I didn't feel the slightest bit guilty any more. I felt pleased with myself because, in a roundabout way, I'd personally donated twenty pence to charity (or will have done when the tights are sold), which can't be a bad thing, right? I mean, I know it's not a lot of money, but in the store I took them from the pack of tights was on sale for two pounds fifty, and I bet they didn't cost half that much to produce. My dad told me that shops massively mark up the prices of the things they sell – that's how they can afford to have end of season sales and bargain bins and still make a profit. It's all a giant con. So, if you go into your local charity shop today and you realise you're short of a pair of American tan tights, because you've just laddered yours, or you can't afford two pounds fifty, or maybe you're planning to rob a bank, you might just be lucky and find mine. And I'm sorry if I insulted you by being so mean about them, saying they were ugly and all. But then, I don't suppose that many people who wear American tan tights read blogs. Do they?

Posted by Palgirl at 5:05 PM
Comments: 0
Followers: 1
Blog Archive
Links

Chapter 3

Ruby and Amanda trawled the high street for hours. They weren't conscious of it, but over the years they had developed a pattern, a trail through the shops that they habitually followed, like ants making their way across a house. Some shops they marched straight into, while at others they stopped merely to gaze in the windows before moving on. Many didn't merit a single glance. They snaked up the road, crossing backwards and forwards, sometimes doubling back on themselves, and all the while chatting and giggling. Most of their conversations were broken, their sentences interrupted by cries of, 'Look, there's a sale on at . . .' or 'I *love* that dress!' but neither of them minded; it was taken as read that they'd only half listen to each other. They'd have a proper chat later, over burgers and milkshakes.

They took armfuls of clothes into changing rooms and preened in front of mirrors trying on hats and hair slides, but they bought very little. Amanda couldn't find any jeans that fitted right, so she treated herself to a studded belt that she found in a bargain bin at her favourite boutique, while Ruby bought a scarf decorated with pink butterflies. They made mental notes about what they'd come back for when they received their monthly allowances, but Ruby knew that if she really wanted something she had only to ask her dad for it. She couldn't remember the last time she'd had to save up, or wait, for anything. Weirdly, she thought, she missed the sense of anticipation, the thrill of waking up on a Saturday morning knowing that she would finally be able to acquire the object of her lust.

Shopping is a tiring business. Once, as an experiment, Amanda had worn a pedometer, one of those wristbands that counts your footsteps, during a particularly vigorous shopping trip, and at the end she calculated that they had covered six miles in a single afternoon. 'They should let us go shopping instead of doing PE,' Ruby had said, and she was only half joking. That afternoon's shopping trip was particularly tiring for Amanda, because she'd insisted on wearing her new platform heels, instead of her usual trainers. Her feet were covered in blisters which, oddly, only seemed to hurt when she was walking on the pavement; once inside a shop she'd spy something she liked and launch herself towards it, her limp vanishing miraculously. Anaesthetised by the lure of a new dress or bag, she'd forget all about the pain of her blisters until she was out on the street again. Ruby suggested that they go to Boots to buy some plasters for her, but Amanda said they were running out of time and the shops – the good shops – would be closing soon.

'You know what?' said Ruby, studying her watch. 'You can cut your feet to shreds if you want, but I really do want to go to Boots. And it closes in half an hour.' She'd remembered that she needed to buy a new mascara because the one she'd been using was drying up and flaking all over her cheeks, like black dandruff.

'Fine,' said Amanda, her limp becoming more pronounced at the thought. 'I'm in agony. I think there's actual blood in my shoes. Gross.'

Once they were in Boots, Ruby left Amanda to try on some new lipsticks, while she went to get her mascara. She intended to pick up her usual brand, until she noticed that displayed alongside it was a brand new formulation in a bright purple tube. Not only was it on special offer, but it also promised to quadruple the size of your lashes (hers only doubled them) and to last for up to twenty-four hours without smudging or flaking. It was called 'Dynamite Lashes', a name which Ruby thought bizarre. Who wants their lashes to explode? She giggled as she imagined herself at a party, wowing the other guests . . . *And now, prepare to be amazed, astounded and showered in black fibres . . . Witness my amazing exploding lashes!* She decided to buy it, even though it was a pound more than her usual brand, just because it appeared to offer so much more. She took her new mascara to the checkout, passing Amanda who, shoes kicked to one side, was kneeling by a display, daubing the back of her hands in different shades of lipstick. Ruby guessed her friend hadn't bothered to find herself any blister plasters and wondered if she should buy them for her. She was considerate enough to look, but they cost five pounds and so she thought better of it. Clearly, Amanda's feet couldn't hurt that much, or she'd have found them for herself, wouldn't she?

'Hey, so what do you think of this colour?' said Amanda, when Ruby came back from the checkout. She pouted strawberry pink.

'Cool,' said Ruby. 'Suits you.'

Amanda grinned. 'Thanks. I thought so.'

'You gonna buy it?'

'Nah, I've run out of cash.'

'Come on then. We've got time for one more shop.'

Amanda got to her feet and blotted her lips with the back of her hand, before trying to wipe away the greasy lipstick marks with a bit of cotton wool. Her hands were still stained with blotches of pink and red. Self-consciously, she pulled her sleeves down to cover them. As they walked to the exit, she grimaced with the pain of her blisters and muttered something about plasters. She was fishing for sympathy again but Ruby pretended not to have heard.

'Are you hungry?' Ruby asked.

'Yes, I'm —'

BEEP! BEEP! BEEP! BEEP! BEEP! BEEP!

'Shit!' said Amanda, under her breath.

BEEP! BEEP! BEEP! BEEP! BEEP! BEEP! BEEP! BEEP! BEEP! BEEP! BEEP! BEEP! BEEP!

Ruby hesitated, unsure whether to keep going through the exit doors or to hang back. The noise was shrill and relentless and the security barrier was flashing manically in time to it. *BEEP! BEEP! BEEP! BEEP! BEEP!* She stepped backwards into the shop and the sound and light show abruptly ceased. 'Great,' she muttered, her heart rate increasing rapidly. 'Why does stuff like this always happen to me?'

'Excuse me, miss.' The security guard had materialised at Ruby's side. Tall and broad, he was expressionless and apparently emotionless. He reminded Ruby of the soldiers who guard the Royal Family, the ones in the ridiculous bearskin hats, who won't smile for your photos and don't flinch if you tease them. 'Can I check your bag please, miss?' he asked, in a monotone. He didn't look her in the eye.

Ruby nodded and tried to smile innocently, but she felt breathless and her cheeks were glowing hot. She stared at the floor, certain everyone was looking at her, curiously guilty, even though she had absolutely nothing to feel guilty about. 'I've got the receipt,' she said, fumbling in her coat pocket for it.

He barely glanced at it. 'I'm sure you have. It's just a formality, miss.' The security guard opened her bag and took a cursory look inside, pushing his fingers into the inside pockets. Ruby hoped he didn't accidentally touch the shreds of tissue or the bits of old boiled sweet that she'd meant to throw away. Not that he'd react if he did, she was sure. He removed the plastic bag containing her new mascara from her handbag, and took the tube out to examine it. 'See here,' he said pointing to a tab on the side. 'They haven't scanned this properly. Happens a lot. Take it back to the counter and ask them to do it for you.'

Ruby tutted and rolled her eyes. She didn't like being made to feel like a criminal when it was someone else's fault. 'OK.' She asked Amanda to wait for her outside while the offending tag was rescanned. There was a queue at the checkout, but she didn't see why she should join it and so she pushed her way straight to the front. The assistant was apologetic but, Ruby thought, not apologetic enough. She didn't look much older than Ruby; it was probably just her Saturday job.

As they walked away from the shop, Amanda exhaled noisily. 'Phew!' she said. Then she giggled. 'For a second there I thought that was me.'

'What do you mean?'

'I thought I'd got caught.'

'Caught for what?'

Amanda reached into her jacket pocket and pulled something out. It was a slightly tarnished gold tube. Grinning, she unscrewed the lid and swivelled up the creamy, pink stick from within: the exact shade of strawberry that she'd admired on her lips, but didn't have the money to buy.

Ruby laughed, from surprise, not because she found it funny. 'You nicked the tester?' she exclaimed.

'Yeah, I took it while you were queuing to pay for your mascara. I checked no one was watching and I was on the floor so I don't think the cameras could see me.'

'Mand!'

'Why not? It's not like they were going to sell it. It didn't have a price on it. Testers are like pens and lighters – they don't belong to anyone in particular. They're everyone's, aren't they? Communal property.'

'I think that's gross. Do you know how many people have tried that lipstick? They'll have cold sores and chapped lips and all kinds.'

'Yeah, but I'll just cut the top bit off and give it a wipe. It'll be fine.'

Ruby pursed her lips into an expression of disgust. She remembered how irritating it was when she wanted to try some make-up and the tester was missing. 'It's not just that,' she said. 'Nobody else will be able to try that colour now. So you've actually stopped it being everyone's.'

Unrepentant, Amanda smirked. 'Good. I don't want everyone to be wearing the same lippie as me, do I?'

Ruby shrugged. She felt annoyed with Amanda, but she couldn't explain why. There was just something a little bit skanky, a little bit selfish, about stealing a tester. Ruby knew that Amanda could be thoughtless sometimes, that she didn't always think about other people's feelings, and it upset her. Amanda was a good mate in many ways, but she was also the type of girl who didn't care whether you'd fancied a boy for three years, but were too shy to make a move. She'd steam on in there and snog him, if she wanted to, and then seem bemused when you got upset. She'd done it to Ruby twice over the years, and she didn't even really like either boy that much. But Ruby knew she couldn't say anything about that – what did it have to do with lipstick, after all – and so, sighing, she changed the subject. 'Where to next?'

'New Look?' suggested Amanda. 'They've got some great new shoes in.'

Ruby couldn't resist. 'OK, as long as you don't nick the tester shoe.'

'No point,' said Amanda. 'What would I do with one shoe?'

Hop, thought Ruby, although she didn't say it.

Chapter 4

On Tuesday morning, Ruby and Noah walked out of their front doors at exactly the same moment. Unless one of them had been extremely rude, there was absolutely no way they could have avoided meeting on the street outside. Noah was pleased to have another excuse to talk to Ruby. He hadn't intended to bump into her, honestly. He hadn't been peering through the glass in the front door, timing his exit to coincide with hers; it really was just a happy accident. And, given that they lived in the same street and went to the same school, which started at the same time every day, there was a certain inevitability about it. It was a wonder it didn't happen more often. That it didn't was only because Ruby was almost always running later than Noah, delayed by whatever it is that takes girls so long to do in the mornings.

'Hi Ruby,' he said, smiling broadly. He hoped he

didn't appear too excited to see her.

'All right, Noah,' she replied, in a cool tone which made Noah certain she didn't feel the same. She swung her bag on to her other shoulder, which meant he couldn't walk close to her. He wondered if she'd done it deliberately.

He fumbled for something to say. 'So, did your friend sort out her blog then?' he asked.

'I, er . . . dunno.' She hesitated. 'Not yet.'

'Oh, it's just that . . . I thought . . . Oh right,' he said. 'Well, let me know if she needs any more advice.'

'Yeah, I will do. Thanks again for the other day.'

'Don't mention it,' he said. There was a pause. 'So, uh, what you doing today?'

The look she gave him made him feel stupid. 'Going to school, like you, I guess. It's a Tuesday, we don't really have any choice, do we?'

He tried to rescue himself. 'Yes, I know, obviously. I mean, like, after school. I heard there were auditions for the choir, or something. You sing, don't you?'

'Yeah,' she said. 'A bit. But I wasn't planning to go. Choir isn't really my thing.'

'Oh,' he said. 'You should go. You've got a really nice voice.'

She blushed. 'No I haven't, not really. Anyway, when did you hear me sing?'

He wanted to say, 'You're always singing under your breath, when you don't think anyone can hear, when you're walking along with your iPod or waiting outside your house,' but how could he tell her that he'd taken that much notice? 'Probably when we were about ten,' he said.

She smiled. 'Oh right, well that was quite a long time ago. What was I singing, "The Wheels on the Bus" or something?' She giggled. 'I hope I don't sing like that now.'

'Still . . . ' he said. There was another silence. 'I'm learning how you can record music, you know. On my PC, I mean.' She hadn't asked, but he thought it might make him sound more interesting to her.

'Oh, I see. I don't know anything about recording stuff. Or computers. But you already know that!'

'I'll show you some time if you like,' he said. It came out before he could stop himself and he felt a wave of heat spread upwards from his neck to his ears. 'I don't mean . . . '

He could tell she wasn't really listening, anyway. She'd slowed down a little and appeared to be hanging back from him. 'Sorry, Noah, but I said I'd meet Hanni. She lives just over there, so I'd better go. Sorry. See you later, OK?'

He couldn't hide his disappointment. 'Sure,' he said flatly. 'Of course you do. I guess I'll see you around then?'

She nodded, but she was looking in the other direction. 'OK, then, bye.'

Noah opened his mouth to say 'Bye' too, then shut it

again wordlessly, when he noticed that Ruby was already out of earshot. I must look like a dumb trout, he thought. Pathetic. He made his way to school alone, as usual.

Chapter 5

Ruby waited until Noah had walked out of sight before
knocking on Hanni's front door. She'd barely taken her
hand away when it opened.

'I saw you through the window!' Hanni said,
embracing her friend. She insisted on kissing everyone
three times, something she'd seen in a foreign film.
'Who was that guy you were with? Didn't look like
Ross.' She widened her eyes. 'Don't tell me! Was that
nerdy Noah?'

'Yes,' said Ruby, embarrassed that they'd been
spotted. She started walking, so that Hanni had to catch
her up. 'But don't take the piss, OK? He's all right,
really.' She thought she'd better qualify her statement.
'For a geek, I mean.'

'If you say so,' said Hanni.

'I do. Anyway, he sorted out my computer for me. If

it weren't for him I wouldn't have been able to chat to you online every night.'

'Ooh! Touchy, touchy. OK!' She hesitated. 'Talking of computers, what's happening with your blog? You were going to tell me when you'd written something. I'm dying to see it.'

Ruby screwed up her face. 'I decided not to do one. I mean, I couldn't think of anything to write about in the end. Waste of time.'

Hanni nodded. 'Funny, me neither. I sat down to do it and then I just thought, what's the point?'

'Mand hasn't started hers either. Don't know about anyone else. We're all crap, really.'

'Yeah, but who's got the time? And if people find out you're writing one they only go on it and write bitchy comments on it or print it out and pass it around so everyone can laugh at you. Remember that girl in the year above? She got bullied for her blog. She had to take it down in the end.'

'Yeah,' said Ruby. She shrugged. 'It was a stupid idea.'

By now they were approaching the school gates and there were hundreds of other pupils walking with them. Ruby looked around her and realised she didn't recognise anybody at all. She thought how weird it was that you could spend four years of your life in the same place as so many other people, share experiences and memories with them, and yet never speak to them or learn their names. That was the thing about going to such a big school, she supposed. Her dad had wanted her to go to the small, private school nearby, but her mum had disagreed, and because she was the one who looked after Ruby full-time, she got her way. Ruby wondered what life would be like now if she had gone to St Catherine's. She often saw the girls, with their green uniforms and neat ponytails, and she tried to imagine herself as one of them. Would she be a different person? Would she speak differently? Who might her friends be?

'Double science today,' said Hanni, interrupting her thoughts.

'Mmm . . . '

'And we've got that careers thing.'

'Yeah. Have you decided on your work experience yet?'

'No. Don't mind what I do, as long as I don't have to wear a uniform or work in a factory. Who cares, right?' Hanni shrugged. 'It's not like it's really going to help anyone get a job. Anyway, I'm not going to need a job, am I? Not after I've become super-famous.'

'Yeah, maybe you could get some work experience with Simon Cowell.'

Hanni laughed. 'You know, that's not such a bad idea. I might suggest that. I could help him write his put-downs, or become a new judge. Ha! What about you?'

Ruby shook her head. 'No clue,' she said. It was so easy when she was little. She was so confident that she wanted to be a vet, and then it was a singer, and then an actress. There was even a short period at primary school when she'd wanted to become a lollipop lady because she'd liked the idea of carting around a giant lollipop. And now? All she knew was that she wanted to be a 'somebody'. But, unlike Hanni, she didn't want to be famous for going on some reality TV show. She wanted to be famous for *something*.

Some people were so lucky. They knew what they were good at, they loved doing it and they could be certain they'd want to do it for the rest of their lives. Ruby thought of herself as average: fairly, but not spectacularly, good at most things. She was pretty, but no prettier than thousands of other girls, and she was averagely popular, averagely clever and averagely funny, with average-sized feet and average-sized boobs. What do average people do when they leave school? They have average lives and average jobs and average families. Ruby knew that would never be enough for her. 'I've got absolutely no clue,' she repeated. 'I guess I'll take whatever they offer me.'

Ross was waiting for Ruby in the corridor outside her classroom. Ruby nodded at him, self-consciously. He smiled, came up behind her and put his arms around her waist. He didn't do it in an affectionate way, but in a way that said, 'Hands off, she's mine,' to anyone who might be watching. 'Looking good,' he said, approvingly, in the way you might admire a flashy car. He said it loud enough so that his mates could hear. 'Maybe see you later.'

'Maybe,' Ruby said, embarrassed and uncomfortable. She stepped away from him and walked into the classroom, heading straight to the back, where she and Hanni always sat with their friends. There was just time for a brief catch-up before the school day started. The Head had done away with assemblies, except on Mondays and on the last day of term, and so, after the register, it was straight into lessons.

The science teacher, Mrs Brockhurst, was a large, miserable-looking woman who didn't appear to like children very much. Amanda swore she was a sadist who got a kick out of humiliating kids. Why else would she give everyone their tests back in order of how badly you'd done, so you knew that the longer you waited for yours, the more likely you were to have failed, and everybody else could see how stupid you were? Not that Ruby worried about failing. She found science dull but doable, and she could have put money on the fact she'd come twelfth or thirteenth (out of thirty-six) in the test, a few places before Amanda. Hanni was the one who always flunked, but she didn't care. She wore her failure like a badge of honour, appearing disappointed if anybody did worse than her. That day was no different. Ruby came thirteenth and Amanda fifteenth. Hanni came thirty-sixth, presumably because she hadn't bothered to turn up for the test at all.

After science, there was English, and after lunch, history and maths. Ruby got through them all on autopilot, by half listening and half concentrating, while she, Hanni and Amanda passed silly notes back and forth, discussing the teachers and the boys in their year. As long as they didn't giggle too much the teachers didn't appear to notice them. Who cared if they were actually learning anything?

Throughout that week, everybody in the year was being called out of class to go to see the careers adviser, Miss Duncan, about their work experience placements. Ruby looked forward to her appointment all afternoon, not because she was keen to discuss her placement, but because it would break up the day and ease the monotony. It was almost three-thirty by the time she was called in. She'd never met Miss Duncan before and she was surprised to see how young she looked, not much older than a sixth former. What a weird job careers adviser was, she thought. Miss Duncan spent her days helping other people decide on their future careers, when she'd almost certainly never tried any of them herself. In all likelihood, Ruby decided, Miss Duncan had become a careers adviser because she hadn't worked out what else she wanted to do.

'So, Ruby,' said Miss Duncan. 'Any idea of where you might like us to place you?'

'Nope, sorry.'

Miss Duncan sighed. 'Right. Do you know what you might like to do when you leave school, after sixth form?'

'Not really.'

Miss Duncan seemed disappointed, although not surprised. She looked through Ruby's school record. 'You get decent marks. I assume you'll be thinking about university. How about law or business?'

Ruby shook her head. She didn't want to spend her placement bored out of her brain in a stuffy office with a bunch of people in suits, filing paperwork. She wondered what would happen if she was cheeky and said, 'Do you know what? My ultimate ambition is to be a careers adviser at this school', but she didn't think Miss Duncan had much of a sense of humour.

'OK, then. So what do you like doing, Ruby?'

Ruby thought about it. She liked hanging out with her friends, surfing the web and watching TV. Oh, and reading magazines. 'I like reading,' she said, because it sounded better.

'Hmm,' said Miss Duncan, leafing through a pile of paperwork on her desk. 'I don't think we have anything suitable.' She chewed her pen. 'Anything else you enjoy?'

'Going shopping,' said Ruby. She qualified it: 'I like fashion.'

'Ah, retail.' Her voice sounded brighter. 'Yes, we might be able to find a work experience placement for you in retail.' She scribbled something on a list. 'Thank you, Ruby. Leave it with me and I'll get back to you.'

Ruby hesitated. Was that it? Her future career decided? Because she liked shopping? She hovered above her chair, hoping that Miss Duncan would suddenly remember she had an exciting placement that might be perfect for her, doing something she'd never thought of, but at which she'd excel.

'You can go back to your form now, Ruby.'

'Oh, right, um, thanks.'

A girl called Lily Lawton, whom she vaguely knew from her French class, was sitting in the waiting area outside Miss Duncan's office. She gave her a sympathetic smile.

'Was it OK?' Lily asked.

'Sure,' said Ruby. 'It was pretty much how I thought it would be. Here's a tip: I'd make up a really bizarre hobby, like witchcraft or something, if I were you.'

On her way back to the classroom Ruby passed the noticeboard where you could sign up to audition for the school choir. She stopped to look at it. Maybe Noah was right. Maybe she should put her name down. Singing was such a brilliant way to let off steam and it would be good to have a big concert to look forward to, something that both her parents would have to come to together. She might even get to sing a solo. Inspired by a sudden burst of enthusiasm, she picked up the pencil, which was attached to the board by a piece of string, and read down the list of names, intending to add hers to the bottom. But when she realised she didn't know a single person who'd signed up, and thought about what her friends would say, she changed her mind and walked away, leaving the pencil swinging forlornly.

Now she felt flat and empty, like there wasn't any point to anything. She looked at her watch. It was virtually the end of the day, but she couldn't face going back to class and she didn't feel like hanging out with her friends after school, especially if Ross was going to be there. Instead, she fetched her coat from her locker in the cloakroom, swung her bag over her shoulder and brazenly exited the school through the main doors. There was no one around to question or to stop her; they were either still in lessons or had already left.

She couldn't be bothered to walk, so she caught the bus from the end of the road, but got off two stops early, on the high street. She wandered up and down for a while, looking aimlessly in shop windows, as if she couldn't make up her mind where she wanted to go or what she wanted to do. And then, on a mannequin, in the window of the department store, she found what she was looking for. It was a long, sparkling chain made up of interlinking sections. The necklace was so colourful and so enticing, it seemed the perfect antidote to her boring, grey, pointless day.

Once she was inside, it didn't take her long to find the object of her desire. It was hanging from a hook on the wall in the accessories section, alongside three other necklaces. Carefully, she took it off the hook and held it up to the lights, and it sparkled red and green and pink, as if the metal had a rainbow running through it. She didn't look at the price, although she knew it must be expensive. Excitement welled up within her. Her heart was pounding so fast and so loud that she felt dizzy. It was a wonder that nobody else could hear it.

She examined the necklace, quickly. Whoever had put the security tag on had done so without attention or care. All she had to do to free the necklace from its packaging was to unhook the clasp and pull it, link by link, through a cardboard hook. In just a few seconds, it had slipped out and lay coiled in her right hand. She closed her palm over it, enjoying, for a moment, the sensation of the cold, smooth metal against her skin. Then she took a deep breath and glanced around her. When she was sure that nobody was looking in her direction, she let the necklace fall into her bag through a small gap at the top. There was a soft rustling sound as it uncoiled on its way down. Swinging her bag across her shoulder once again, she turned and strode purposefully to the exit doors, marching straight across the pedestrian crossing outside. It was only when she reached the other side of the road that she remembered to exhale.

My Blog

January 28

Whoops, I did it again.

OK, I'll admit it wasn't an accident, but I didn't exactly plan it, either. It just happened, the way things you have some control over, but also know are inevitable, happen. The first time was so easy and it made me feel so good – for a short while, at least – that I had to repeat the experience. I just had to. It was like visiting a fairground and finding yourself in the queue for the biggest, scariest ride there is, knowing that you're going to be terrified out of your mind, but waiting in line and getting on it anyway, because you also know you're about to enjoy a thrill like no other. And then the barriers come down, and it's too late to change your mind, and you're away! You scream all the way through, begging somebody, anybody, to stop the ride so you can get off. You're dizzy and sick and certain you're only seconds away from death. But when the ride ends, you feel exhilarated, alive, like you're invincible. And the moment you climb off, and your excitement fades, you're dying to get straight back on again.

Most of the time, my life is flat. Routine is like gravity, with heavy chains which pull me back and tie me down. When I steal I feel lifted. I feel taller, bigger, stronger. I feel like I'm flying free.

I was on my way home from school, and I was feeling miserable and empty, and I didn't want to go home yet, not like I did every other boring day. Instead, I found myself heading to the shops, half aware of what I was going to do, but not allowing myself to put it into words. It was a bit like having an itch that needed to be scratched, but in a place I couldn't reach. An itch on the inside. I wandered past the shops, hoping that something would call to me, asking to be taken, just as the tights had done. This time, I wanted it to be better than tights, more appealing and more expensive. You see, I figured that if a pair of nasty tights could make me feel that good, how much better might I feel if I took something I really liked, something I might want? And how much more grateful would the charity shop be to receive something that people would want to buy? I knew even before I did it that I wasn't going to keep whatever I took, that it was never going to be mine. It was all about the taking, not the keeping. Giving it away would stop the stealing being a bad thing and make it into a good thing. Well, maybe not exactly a good thing, but a less bad one, at any rate.

I soon found it in the window of a clothes shop that I liked, but couldn't afford to shop in, the type of place my dad might take me to if he wanted to buy me a treat. It was a necklace, hanging from the unfeasibly long plastic neck of a mannequin, and as soon as I saw it, all sparkly and pretty and stupidly expensive, the adrenalin started pumping through my body, and I knew I'd found my prize. I also knew it would be both easy to take and easy to hide. I did my coat up to the top, so you couldn't see my school uniform underneath, and walked in with as much confidence as I could muster. Luck was on my side. There was only one shop assistant, and she was helping somebody at the till; I don't think she even registered that I'd come in. I was in and out within thirty seconds, like a cartoon phantom, so fast that I probably left skid marks in the carpet.

I popped home before I went to the charity shop. I needed to calm down first and I thought it would look a bit suspect if I brought in just one new-looking item again. The necklace really didn't seem like something a poor, dead gran would wear, so I dug out a couple of Mum's old jumpers from the spare room, and bundled everything into a tatty plastic bag.

'Hello again dear,' said the same volunteer, when I walked in. 'How nice to see you.'

'Thanks,' I said. 'You too. I've brought in some more stuff. We had a bit of a clear out at home.'

She emptied my plastic bag on to the counter. The necklace glittered pleasingly, and for a moment I wanted to keep it for myself. I even thought about saying I'd made a mistake and it shouldn't have been in with the jumpers.

The volunteer's beaming smile changed my mind. 'Thank you dear, what a lovely piece. It looks almost brand new. So shiny. Lovely.'

'Oh, I gave it a bit of a polish for you,' I said, delighted that she seemed so happy with my donation. I felt warm inside, like I'd just helped a blind person to cross the road. 'I got it for my birthday but I never wear it.'

'Thank you. People don't tend to bring us much jewellery these days, they put it on eBay instead. It'll look lovely in the window display. And thank you for the jumpers too. We do well with patterned knitwear, especially when it's pure lambswool. The mature ladies like it.'

'Great,' I said. 'They're my mum's.' I didn't say she only wore them when she was cleaning the windows and didn't want to spoil her decent clothes. Or that she didn't know I'd donated them.

She took her price list and her book of labels from under the counter and examined the jumpers. 'I think we can get about three pounds for each of these,' she said. Then she held up the necklace again and peered at it through her reading glasses. 'It is lovely, but it's only costume jewellery.' '£1.50' she wrote on a label, which she stuck on to the clasp at the back.

'No!' I wanted to shout, dismayed at her ignorance. How could she work in a shop and be so clueless about what things cost? No wonder people put stuff on eBay. 'You can't charge that little for it! That's like stealing from the charity! It's brand new and it's on sale up the road right now for sixty quid!' But of course I couldn't. So I gritted my teeth and smiled and said I really hoped that someone nice bought it. And then I went home and did my coursework.

Posted by Palgirl at 7:05 PM
Comments: 0
Followers: 1
Blog Archive
Links

Chapter 6

Ruby was a natural at shoplifting, she'd discovered. She had a talent for it. Maybe it was because she'd been told she possessed what people called an 'honest' or 'open' face, whatever that means, but nobody ever seemed to suspect that she was up to no good. She could walk into a shop, browse for a few minutes, take whatever she pleased, and then leave, as if it was the most natural thing in the world – as if handing over money had no place in the normal shopping experience. The more she practised, the more adept she became. She was like a magician, able to secrete items inside her bag, or her coat, with the merest flutter of her fingers. It was easy, if you knew what to take and what to avoid, if you were aware of the cameras and the security guards and the alarms. The key was to look confident and purposeful, even, if you were brazen enough, to smile at the assistants and have a little chat with them, so they let their guard down. It was like acting, really. Sometimes, Ruby would buy one – usually very cheap – item and steal something more expensive at the same time. It was her version of buy one get one free.

Although her first few shoplifting expeditions had been spontaneous, impulsive acts, which happened because she was upset, she soon learned it was preferable if she did it when she was calm and in control. If she was feeling emotional she was more likely to make mistakes, to be clumsy or not to concentrate properly. And that, she reasoned, was when she might get caught. Weirdly, though, she'd noticed she didn't feel upset very often any more; things didn't seem to get to her the way they used to, not when she knew it was only ever a few hours until her next outing. She let unhappy feelings wash over her, numbly, as if they belonged to somebody else. Now, there was only the high of a successful steal and the dull ache until she did it again.

Without their knowledge (of course), she had begun to steal to order for the charity shops. Whenever she donated something – and she had taken to visiting several different shops, so as not to arouse suspicion – she would chat to the grateful assistant to find out what items sold the best and what could get the highest price. Jewellery, they told her, was always a popular seller, as were books, scarves and cashmere jumpers. While these were all fairly easy to steal, other charity shop favourites like jackets and coats were a no-go for Ruby, because they were virtually impossible to hide.

It amazed her how lax many shops were, forgetting to put tags on things, or putting them on so poorly that you could pull them off with barely any effort. It was almost as if they were asking you to shoplift. So convinced was Ruby of her own skill, and so confident was she of her growing experience, that she soon began to forget how much luck was involved too. And that, as she would discover one Saturday afternoon a few weeks into her new career, was dangerous.

She was in her local department store, Kelly's, a favourite shoplifting haunt because it was big and well-stocked and the ratio of shop staff to customers was very low. Not to mention that it had everything a charity shop could possibly want. She had scoped it out, noticing on which points the security cameras were focused and what paths the two security guards took. They were like mice, she'd noticed, always following the same pattern. She had bided her time, browsing in the accessories department, picking things up, examining them and then putting them down again, as if she couldn't quite decide on a gift for somebody. Today she was looking at silk scarves, which had just come in as part of the store's new spring collection. They were the sort of thing her mother might like, or her aunt – soft and floaty, in muted beiges and greys. Today it would be easy: the store had given her a helping hand. Stupidly, no doubt to protect the silk, the security tags had been attached not to the scarves but to the scarves' labels, which were sewn on with only a few stitches. Ruby could see immediately that they would come away with a simple tug.

When she was as sure as she could be that nobody was watching her, she picked up two scarves in exactly the same colour and took them over to the full-length mirror nearby. She wrapped one around her neck and pirouetted around, as if she was admiring her reflection. As she did this, she tore the tagged label from the other scarf and let it drop to the floor, gently kicking it under the mirror with her foot. Perhaps her de-tagging was a little too violent, because it left a small hole, but that was fine for the purposes of the charity shop. It made the scarf look more authentically secondhand; she could even say it was moth-eaten. And then, in one brisk movement, as she unwrapped the first scarf from around her neck, she used her other hand to stuff the second, now tag-less scarf in her coat pocket. Slowly, diligently, she walked back over to the display table and replaced the first scarf in the pile, as though she'd decided it simply wasn't to her taste. She might have looked calm, but she was breathless, her heart drilling into her chest wall and the blood pumping hot in her cheeks and ears. She loitered a while, pretending to examine a few other items, as she tried to bring her breathing back to normal, and then, with a determined stride, she made for the exit.

The doors were only a few metres away. Just a few more steps . . .

'Stop!'

Someone had her arm. Ruby's insides seized up, although somehow her legs kept walking of their own accord. It was a strange sensation, a bit like taking your feet off the pedals when you're cycling downhill, she thought. So this was it. *This was it.* She had always imagined that if she got caught she'd feel a tight, vice-like grip around her wrist. She'd expected that it would hurt, like a handcuff or a Chinese burn. But the hand on her arm was far gentler than she had anticipated. She felt only the light brush of long fingers, a touch that felt almost affectionate. As she quickened her pace she could sense the figure of a man looming behind her, walking at exactly the same pace, his hand still grasping for her arm.

'Ruby,' he said. 'Please stop.'

That was odd.

'How do you know my name?' she asked. She felt weirdly, unexpectedly calm. She turned her head round slowly to face the man.

It wasn't a security guard. It wasn't a man at all, just a very tall boy. It was Noah.

'What the hell?'

'Just stop please, OK?' he said. If the voice hadn't sounded familiar, it was because it was deeper than she recalled.

'But I —'

'Shush,' whispered Noah. He was shaky and very red in the face. 'Don't say anything and don't look behind you, but the security guy has clocked you and he's been following you around for a couple of minutes.'

'What do you mean?' she asked. She realised her legs had stopped walking, although she couldn't remember telling them to. Now her feet were stuck fast to the floor, while everything around her seemed to be spinning faster and faster. How was it possible that she hadn't noticed the brightness of the lights before? How had she been unaware of the music and the low purr of chatter that wove its way through it? It was as if she'd been brought suddenly out of a trance.

'He saw you take that scarf and he's waiting for you to leave the store,' Noah said. 'I saw him talking into his radio about you.'

Ruby giggled, involuntarily. The weird, raspy noise that erupted from her didn't even sound like her normal laugh. She thought of saying, 'What scarf? I don't know what you're talking about' or 'It was an accident' but she knew it would sound pathetic. 'I, uh . . . ' she stuttered. She felt sick and wobbly. She tried again: 'I, didn't, uh . . . ' She stared straight ahead. Perhaps if she didn't look at Noah she could pretend this wasn't happening. For a moment, she wondered if being arrested might be preferable. At least a security guard or a policeman wouldn't know her, or live in her street.

'You've got to put the scarf back,' Noah said, as

firmly as he could. 'And, if there's anything else you've taken, you've got to put that back too. He's waiting for you to go outside so he can stop you and arrest you. That's how they work.'

'I . . . I . . . don't know what to do,' she stuttered. She felt she was on the brink of tears, but didn't want to cry in front of Noah.

'It's OK,' he said. 'Just go back over to the scarf table and take it out of your pocket and leave it there. If you go out the shop and you haven't taken anything, it's not shoplifting, is it?'

Ruby shook her head.

'So I'll wait here for you and then we'll leave together, OK?'

Ruby nodded. 'OK,' she whispered. She wasn't convinced that she could do it. Maybe, she thought, if I pray really hard, or click my heels three times, or say a magic word, I can make myself disappear instead.

Chapter 7

Noah watched as Ruby walked back through the shop to the table on which the scarves were neatly piled. Her head was bowed, her steps an uneven shuffle. He hadn't seen Ruby appear so fragile, or so lacking in confidence, at least not since they were little. She looked crestfallen, just like she always used to when they were about six and her dad told her off for lying or being cheeky. He couldn't explain why, but if he tried not to think about the fact she was a thief, her vulnerability made her even more attractive. It made him feel stronger too, like he was in control for once, like he mattered to her. He felt he wanted to protect her.

Ruby had almost reached the table when he saw the security guard, heading straight for her, his radio to his ear. He realised with alarm that Ruby, her back to him, still had the scarf in her pocket. He had to do something. He had to do something fast. 'Think! Think!' he repeated under his breath. He launched himself across the shop with such speed that he was able to double back on himself and block the security guard's path to the table. 'Excuse me,' he said. 'Can you tell me where the nearest cashpoint is?'

The guard stopped. 'Um, uh, yeah, it's across the road,' he said, distracted, trying to peer past Noah. For once, Noah was glad of his height and the span of his arms.

'Where exactly?'

The security guard sighed. 'Come out of the shop, cross the road and turn left,' he said. 'It's about fifty yards away. You can't miss it.' He started walking away.

'Thanks,' said Noah. He turned around to see Ruby coming towards him, looking nervous. Please Ruby, he thought, as she approached, please have put the scarf back. He stared directly at her, opening his eyes as wide as they would go. Comprehending, she nodded.

But before she could reach him, the guard stopped her. 'Can I see your pockets please, miss?'

'Sure,' she said, forcing a smile. Noah wondered if the guard could tell how nervous she was. She emptied her coat pockets for him, showing him what looked like some chewing gum and an old receipt, and then turned the linings inside out so that it was clear she was concealing nothing.

He nodded. 'Now please open your bag for me,' he said.

Ruby did as she was asked. Noah could see that her

hands were shaking, even though she must have known he wouldn't find anything there. Unless she'd taken something else, something he hadn't seen? Had she?

The guard peered inside. 'Thank you,' he said, sounding disappointed. 'You're free to go.' He glanced suspiciously at Ruby and then at Noah. Perhaps, Noah thought, he was beginning to wonder whether he had been duped. Noah stood still as the guard sized him up, evidently trying to work out if Ruby could have passed him whatever it was he'd seen her take. Were they in it together? Noah didn't carry a bag and he was wearing just a fitted jumper and jeans; there was simply no way he could have hidden anything.

'Let's go,' Noah whispered to Ruby. 'Now!'

They walked briskly to the exit, side by side, neither talking nor looking at one other. Once outside, Ruby grabbed Noah's arm. 'Thank you,' she whispered. 'God, that was close.' She seemed stronger now, exhilarated even. Unselfconsciously, she put her hand to her chest as if she was checking her heart. It must have been racing. Had she enjoyed nearly getting caught, he wondered?

'It was close,' he said, flatly. He wasn't excited at all, just relieved it was over and she was safe. 'Are you OK?'

'Yes, I think so. And hey, thank you. I think you just saved my life.'

Noah blushed. 'Nah, it was nothing.' He grinned awkwardly. 'Don't mention it.' He took a deep breath. It was now or never. 'Fancy a milkshake?' he asked.

Chapter 8

Ruby didn't really want a milkshake but she didn't have the energy to refuse, or, she realised, the inclination. If Noah was her guardian angel, she owed him. Probably a lot more than letting him buy her a milkshake, but it was a start.

She let him take her to the burger bar at the other end of the high street. There was one directly opposite the department store, but she figured he was worried that the security guard might see them in there and have second thoughts about letting Ruby go. He was thoughtful like that, always had been. He found them a table and told Ruby to sit down while he went to fetch the milkshakes. He seemed surprised when she asked for vanilla; maybe it was because when she was little she always used to drink strawberry. Or was it chocolate? She could barely remember. Her insides were still churned up and she knew that whatever flavour she chose, it would be too sweet and too cold. She was starting to get a headache, and the brain freeze from the ice wouldn't help, but she didn't want to seem ungrateful. While she waited for Noah to come back, she went back over everything that had happened, retracing her steps in her head. She'd been certain nobody had seen her take the scarf. How could she have come so close to getting caught without realising it? Thank God Noah had been there. But why *was* he there? How did he know she was in the shop? Had he been following her? Was he really stalking her? The idea made her shiver.

Best to come straight out with it. 'Thanks,' she said, when he arrived back with the milkshakes. 'Look, I don't mean to be a bitch, but I need to ask you something. How did you know I was in Kelly's? Were you following me?

'Not exactly,' he said, unfazed, as if he'd been expecting her to ask. 'I was on the high street buying a computer game and I saw you go into Kelly's. I was going to come in and say hello, but then I twigged what you were going to do, so I stood there for a few minutes and kept a look-out for you, and then I saw the security guard and I thought I should warn you.'

'Oh,' she said, relieved. 'That's OK. I mean, that's nice of you. I don't get how I didn't notice you standing there at all.'

'No,' he said. 'I guess you were concentrating pretty hard.'

'How come you said you knew what I was going to do?' she asked, as it occurred to her. 'Have you followed me before?'

'Not exactly. Not like you think. I've not actually followed you in real life. But I have been reading your blog.'

Ruby flushed. 'Really? You've been reading it?' She felt embarrassed and then annoyed and finally foolish, when she remembered that blogs were designed to be read by other people, even people who knew you. 'How did you know it was mine?'

'I helped set it up for you, remember?'

'Oh yeah.' She giggled. 'But I said it was for a friend. How did you know it was me?'

'I could just tell,' he said. 'It sounded like you. It's a good blog. I've looked at thousands and most are pretty boring. At least you've got something to write about.'

'Yeah,' she said. 'My stupid, pathetic life.'

'Don't say that.'

She shrugged.

'I wanted to tell you the other day, but I wasn't sure how to. Didn't you notice you had a follower? At the end of your blog page there's a bit for comments and followers. You've got just one: me.'

Ruby hadn't noticed. Once she'd written a blog entry she didn't go back and look at it again. She didn't like reading her own words. 'No, I didn't realise.' She hesitated. 'God, Noah, you won't tell anyone, will you?

You won't tell my mum?'

'Of course not. Why would I?'

'I don't know. You must think I'm a terrible person.'

'No,' he said. 'Not terrible. You're . . . normal . . . nice. And we all have secrets, even me.'

He was probably only saying that to make her feel better, she decided. She couldn't imagine what secrets he could possibly have, and she didn't presume to ask him. 'Thanks,' she said. She tried to smile.

'Actually, I think you're a bit like Robin Hood.'

Ruby burst out laughing. 'Robin Hood! I think I'd rather be Maid Marian.'

'No, seriously. You're stealing from the rich and giving to the poor, in your own way. It's not like you're keeping what you nick.'

She imagined herself dressed in green, with a bow and an arrow and a pointy hat. She smiled. 'I guess I kind of am,' she said. She liked thinking of herself as a hero, instead of a villain.

'You've got to be careful, Ruby,' he said. 'I'm not always going to be there to watch your back. Maybe . . . Just be careful, OK.'

'Sure,' she said. 'I might not do it again, anyway.' She knew that was a lie before she'd finished the sentence. She looked out of the window at the darkening sky and wondered if any of her friends had gone past and seen her sitting in the burger bar with Noah. She couldn't quite decide whether or not she cared.

Robyn Hood's Blog

I steal from expensive stores and give to charity shops

February 24

If you're observant, you might have noticed that my blog now has a name. I've christened it . . . at last. Calling it 'My Blog' was getting a bit tired, don't you think? Robyn Hood, that's me. Do you like it? I think it describes me pretty well. Robyn, not Robin, because I'm a girl, if you hadn't already figured that out. While there aren't too many forests or glens or sheriffs, or friars around here, in my own way I'm stealing from the rich and giving the poor, aren't I? (And, for the Robin Hood film-lovers among you, don't forget the first thing I stole was tights!) I'm just updating it, bringing it into the twenty-first century. I'd like to take all the credit for the name, but it was actually someone else's idea, the only other person who knows I'm writing this blog. Of course, if he tells anyone, I'll have to kill him. Slowly.

I like the idea of being a modern-day outlaw, a female bandit. They had them in the Wild West, didn't they? Maybe I should adopt a uniform, or a costume, like Zorro. I could wear a mask and tie my hair up under a hat, so nobody would know I was a girl. And then I could ride around the high street on my horse, spreading fear and panic wherever I went. When I chose a shop to target, I would hold out my gun and say, 'Stand and deliver! Your charity shop donations or your life!' and the shop assistants would quake with fear and give me whatever I wanted. I'd put my loot in a big sack, which I'd swing over my shoulder, and then I'd trot down the street, handing out goodies to the charity volunteers. They'd all stand outside their shops and cheer and clap. And little children would run after me . . .

I know I'm getting a bit carried away here, but let me have my little fantasy. It sure beats school and coursework and exams. It just seems a real shame that I'll never be able to tell my friends or my family what I'm up to.

Posted by Robyn Hood at 8:05 PM
Comments: 1
the investig8tor: Your secret is safe with me.
Followers: 1
Blog Archive
Links

Chapter 9

Noah watched Ruby from his bedroom window, just as he had done many times before. She was sitting on the wall outside her house again, waiting for her dad to pick her up. He knew this for certain because she'd told him the day before, when they had bumped into each other in the street. Since he'd rescued her from the security guard, a couple of weeks before, she always acted as if she was pleased to see him and happy to talk to him, treating him more like a friend and less like an annoyance, although that wasn't always the case when they were at school – there she still gave the impression that she was slightly embarrassed to know him. Much as it hurt him, he pretended not to notice. After all, school was school and nobody was really themselves there.

Perhaps she was thinking about him too, because she

glanced upwards for a moment and waved, which made his tummy do little somersaults. He waved back, but she had already turned away, and she was now doing something with her mobile phone. Texting someone, probably.

He liked being the inspiration for the title of Ruby's blog, and he felt privileged to be the only person in the world to share her secret, but he couldn't help feeling that he was encouraging her shoplifting habit, which he hadn't meant to do. Whenever she saw him now she would tell him what she'd stolen, and which charity shop she'd taken it to, sometimes even before she blogged about it. It made him feel special and important, and he was aware that he responded with enthusiasm and excitement, rather than disapproval. Did that make him a bad person? It wasn't as though he was asking her to steal, or congratulating her on it. And he knew she wasn't a bad person either, just a bit mixed up.

Quite why Ruby stole still made little sense to him, despite his conversations with her, and the fact that he had read her blogs over and over again in an attempt to find some explanation. It was like trying to decipher an invisible code, and Noah, usually good at cracking codes, found his inability to solve this one immensely frustrating. To tell the truth, he found *Ruby* immensely frustrating. Frustrating and captivating and irritating and amazing, all at once. He wasn't used to having so many conflicting and confusing feelings at the same time, and it scared him. Sometimes he wondered if he'd rather go back to the way things were before he knew the truth, when life was simple, but then he and Ruby would be practically strangers again, and he was certain he didn't want that either.

He heard a car pull up outside. Ruby's dad must have arrived. When he looked out of the window again, she was climbing into the front seat and closing the car door beside her. The car sped off down the street, and he sighed and wondered what time she'd be back. She'd told him she wouldn't be staying over; she rarely did these days. Her dad had a new girlfriend, and Ruby didn't like her much. 'The evil stepmother-to-be', she called her, even though, as far as Noah knew, she'd only been on the scene for a few weeks. Noah was glad his parents were still together and that at least he didn't have to worry about things like that. The thought of his dad or his mum – especially his mum – kissing someone else made him cringe. Mind you, the sight of his parents kissing each other was bad enough. He turned back to his computer, but he wasn't in the mood for working on his project. It was reaching the point where it was almost complete and he'd have to tell someone about it, and he wasn't sure who to tell, or who he could trust. Instead, he decided to play a computer game, a Second World War game with hyper-realistic graphics that someone had copied for him, and once he'd mastered that (killing twenty-seven Nazis in record time), he chatted to a couple of friends online. It was so easy to waste a Saturday afternoon.

The next time he saw Ruby, it was dark and after dinner. The rest of his family were watching *The X Factor* together, and because it wasn't his thing he'd excused himself and gone up to his bedroom. He hadn't remembered to close the curtains earlier, so when he sat down at his desk he could still see out on to the street. Ruby was sitting on top of one of the giant dustbins in her front garden, swinging her legs backwards and forwards. He wondered how long she'd been there. She looked more beautiful than ever, he thought, her silhouette illuminated by the street lamp, and a halo of light around her hair. Perhaps it was wishful thinking, but it seemed as if she'd been waiting for him, because the moment she noticed him at the window she jumped down from her perch and walked out into the road towards him. Then she leaned backwards, so that she was staring directly into his window, and she waved. At least, it looked like a wave, at first. On second thoughts, Noah realised that she wasn't saying hello, she was drawing her hand in towards her body, motioning to him. Could she be asking him to come out to her? He opened the window and leaned out. 'Hey, Ruby, do you want me to come down?' he shouted.

She put her finger to her lips to silence him, and nodded, beckoning him again.

He nodded back at her and closed the window, aware that his heart had started beating very fast. 'Just popping out,' he shouted, as he ran downstairs, knowing that nobody would hear him over the noise of the television. Without stopping to grab a jacket, he ran through the hall and straight out of the front door. It was only after he'd closed it behind him that he realised he didn't have his keys.

He'd thought Ruby might be waiting for him outside his house, but she had returned to her dustbin seat in her garden, where he'd first spotted her.

She smiled when she saw him approach. 'Take a pew,' she said, pointing to the other dustbin. 'Thanks loads for coming out. I wasn't sure if you'd see me.'

He sat down next to her. It was surprisingly comfortable. 'You're lucky I did,' he said. 'How long have you been out here for?'

'I dunno. A while. Mum thinks I'm still at Dad's. That's why I'm at the bins. You can't see them from the window. If she comes out, I'll say I just came back and bumped into you outside.'

'Right,' he said, nervously. There was a silence and he felt he had to fill it. 'Hey, remember when we were small and we used to play hide and seek in these bins all the time, and then there was that day in the summer holidays that your mum couldn't find you, and the bin men came, and she got into a huge panic thinking you'd got mangled up in the lorry?'

'Yeah,' said Ruby, giggling. 'I think she even called the council. My dad was frantic too. And I was at your house all the time, thinking I was so clever hiding in the cupboard under the stairs. I couldn't understand why everyone was so angry with me when I finally came out. I'd just got bored waiting to be found.'

'I got into loads of trouble for that too, you know?'

'I didn't realise. Sorry.'

'It's OK, I forgave you. Eventually.'

She smiled. 'Good. Hey, Noah, I've been meaning to ask you. Why are you always sitting there, looking out of your window?'

'I'm not watching out for you, if that's what you think,' he said, not entirely truthfully. She blushed. 'It's just because my desk is by the window. So whenever I'm on my PC you can see me, that's all. And waiting for stuff to download or to render can take forever. It gets really boring, so while I'm waiting I look out the window to see what's going on.'

'Oh,' she said. 'But what exactly do you do on your computer all the time? It can't all be schoolwork.'

'Just stuff,' he said. He didn't know whether he should tell her, whether she'd really be interested, or whether she'd understand. So he played it down. 'You know, just games and programming systems and finding data, things like that.' He saw that she was nodding blankly. 'It's pretty boring, really. Maybe one day I'll tell you about it properly.'

'Oh, right, yeah, thanks.'

'I talk to my mates a lot online too,' he said, worried that he'd made himself sound like a nerd again.

'Yeah, me too,' she said. She paused. 'So, I guess you're probably wondering why I called you down here. There's a reason.'

Noah's pulse quickened. 'Yeah?' What he really wanted her to say was, 'Because I missed you so much and I really needed to be with you' but he knew that was a silly fantasy. Whatever her reason, it wasn't to declare her undying love.

'It's about you know what.'

His heart sank. Of course it was. 'Right.'

'My dad took me to this shop this afternoon. It sold jewellery and scarves and bags and stuff like that. He wanted to get a present for Evil Stepmother and he dragged me there to help him. Because I'm a girl, so supposedly I'll know what she'd like. Like all women are the same. Anyway, that's not important. The thing is, I took something while we were in there. It just sort of happened.'

Noah widened his eyes. 'Ruby! When you were with your dad? What if he'd seen you? What if you'd got caught?'

'Yeah, I know, it was stupid. But all the shop assistants were fussing around him because he looks like he has loads of cash, and nobody was taking any notice of me, and there was no security or anything that I could see, and, I don't know, I just did it. To see if I could.'

He nodded. 'So what did you take?'

She reached into her pocket. 'These. Earrings.' She held them out to him, as if she was asking for his approval. They were delicate-looking, with different-shaped coloured stones hanging down like grapes.

'Nice,' he said. He knew that wasn't the right thing to say. 'I mean, um, I see.'

'The thing is, when he brought me home I got him to drop me off on the high street and I tried three different charity shops, but none of them will take earrings for pierced ears. They said it's not hygienic because of hepatitis or HIV or something, and they can't sell them. They're not allowed. So I'm stuck with these brand new earrings that I can't give away, and there's no way I can wear them, obviously, and I don't know what to do with them.'

It dawned on him that she wanted him to help her. 'Right . . . Are you asking me to take them off you?'

She nodded and smiled, expectantly. 'Not for you, obviously. I mean, even if you had your ear pierced, which you don't, they're not really your style. I thought maybe one of your sisters would like them? Or even your mum? As a present. You could say you'd bought them.' She held the earrings out to him again and he studied them.

'They look really expensive,' he said.

'They are,' she said, with perhaps a little too much pride in her voice. 'About a hundred and fifty quid.

They've got real stones in them and they're gold plated. I'd give them to my mum but she'd wonder where I got the money from to buy them, and if she told my dad he might put two and two together.'

'Right, I see.'

'So will you take them?'

'I . . . don't . . . know.' Ruby's face fell and it tugged at his heart. He couldn't bear to disappoint her. 'I mean, I want to help, but I can't give them to my sisters for the same reason,' he said. 'They'd know something was up. I've never bought jewellery for anyone in my life, let alone expensive stuff. It's not even like it's anyone's birthday coming up.'

'Oh,' she said. She looked unhappy.

'And I'd be, like, an accessory,' he said. 'To the crime. For receiving stolen property.' God, now he sounded like he'd watched too many episodes of *The Bill*. 'Can't you just throw them away?'

'I guess I could. And I thought about it. It just doesn't feel right. Someone took hours making these. They're so pretty, someone deserving should have them.'

He didn't really understand but he thought he should try. 'OK, then. But what about putting them away somewhere for now, until you find a good use for them?'

She shrugged. 'I know it's stupid but I don't want them around. I can't explain, but just having them in my room, even hidden away, makes me feel a bit sick.'

'Like the tights?' he said. 'Like what you said in your blog?'

'Yeah,' she said. 'Just like that.'

He shrugged. 'Look, if it makes you happy, I'll take them. I can hide them away and if they're at my place you won't have to worry about them.'

'Really?' she said, in what sounded like mock surprise, as if she'd always known he'd agree in the end. 'That would be brilliant. I mean it. Thank you.' She handed over the earrings and he slipped them into the back pocket of his jeans. He could feel the metal hooks digging into his bottom through the fabric, an uncomfortable reminder of his collusion. Was he her accomplice now? Were they like that couple in the film, Bonnie and Clyde? Except they weren't a couple, were they?

'Hey, look, I'd better go back inside,' said Ruby, jumping down from the bin. 'Sorry, but my mum will be wondering where I am.'

'Yeah,' said Noah, disappointed. He didn't need to jump off the bin because his feet were already touching the floor. He stood up. 'Me too.'

Ruby came towards him, as if she was going to give him a hug, but then appeared to change her mind. She touched him on the arm. 'Thanks so much again. I mean it, thank you!'

Noah patted his back pocket. 'No worries,' he said. Anxiety gnawed at his gut. He had a nagging feeling that no good was going to come from this. No good at all.

Robyn Hood's Blog

I steal from expensive stores and give to charity shops

March 08

The first thing I ever stole was a bar of chocolate, from the newsagent down the road. I was nine years old. I suppose I might have taken something more impressive, like the Crown Jewels, but the security was fairly tight (at the Tower of London – they didn't keep them at my local newsagent) and I didn't want to end up with my head on a spike, or worse. I took the chocolate bar because I could – because it was there – and because I'd never stolen anything before, and I wanted to try it, just to see what it felt like. It was a Wispa bar, the one with holes running through it, and technically, I suppose, half of what I stole was air, which is free anyway, so you could say it was only half a crime.

I might have been just nine, but I knew it was wrong to steal and that there was a chance a great big flash of lightning would appear from the heavens and strike me down dead. That was part of the thrill, I guess, seeing if I could dodge the lightning, finding out whether what my gran, and my mum and dad, and my teachers had all told me was true. I already had an inkling they were lying, just like they'd lied about the tooth fairy and about Father Christmas. Still, I took comfort from the fact that it was a sunny day and I was wearing trainers with rubber soles.

It was a Sunday morning and I'd only recently been allowed to go to the local shop on my own. I revelled in the sense of freedom I felt, just to be able to walk a few metres from home with all that air around me – only me – and the sun on my face. I felt so grown up, fearless, as if I could do anything I wanted. I had a pound coin in my pocket, my weekly sweets allowance, which was generally enough to buy me a chocolate bar, a packet of crisps and some penny chews. I walked into the shop, swinging my arms happily – buying sweets is quite exciting when you're nine – and Mr Shah said, 'Hello, my little friend,' like he always did. I grinned at him, picked some salt and vinegar crisps out of the box by the door, and skipped over to the chocolate counter to make my selection. In those days, I used to run my fingers across all the bars, one by one, as if I was playing an arpeggio on the piano. I liked the smoothness of them, the grooves where the segments were welded together, the slip of the shiny wrappings. It took me ages to choose, even though I nearly always picked the same thing, a milk chocolate bar filled with liquid caramel, which balled up at the corners of my mouth and made my teeth stick together.

The Wispas were right next to the caramel bars, piled high in a neat rectangle, with one extra bar balanced on the top. It seemed lonely, out of place. I picked it up, fully intending to try to squeeze it into the display with the other bars, when instead, I had an instinct to take it for myself. I looked around me. There was no one else in sight, and Mr Shah was behind his counter right round the other side of the display. Could I do it? Should I do it? What might happen to me if I did? The more I considered taking it, the more I wanted to. Don't ask me what I was thinking; I was nine for God's sake, I didn't analyse things, I just followed my gut. And my gut whispered to me, 'Take it, take it.' So I took it. I stuffed it into my pocket and, as calmly as I could, I walked up to the counter to pay for my other goodies.

There was no lightning strike. Just a firm hand on my shoulder. 'What is that in your pocket?' asked Mr Shah.

My heart rate tripled, I could hear it pulsing in my ears. 'Nothing,' I said, smiling bashfully like children do when they're hiding something. Most kids are terrible liars; only grown-ups know how to do it properly.

'Show me,' he said, holding out his hand to me.

'Nothing, I swear.' I covered my pockets with my palms, protectively. Pathetic, I know. Anyone who looked could have seen that the outline of a chocolate bar bulged through the thin cotton of my jacket.

'Don't you lie to me. I know you took some chocolate. I saw

it in the mirror.' He pointed up at the convex mirror above the counter, through which he could view the whole shop. I hadn't noticed it before. It made the room look like it was floating inside a bubble, and when I stepped closer to it, my face grew larger. That, and my nerves, made me want to giggle. I smirked, inappropriately.

'It is not funny,' said Mr Shah, sternly. 'Stealing is a very serious matter.'

'I'm sorry,' I mumbled. Now I felt like I was going to cry. Defeated, my eyes downcast, I took the Wispa out of my pocket and handed it to him.

He placed it on the counter and shook his head at me. I remember that he looked sad, not angry. 'Why did you steal from me, my friend?'

I shrugged. I couldn't answer.

Mr Shah made me stand behind the counter with him while he called my parents. I gazed down at the floor, my chin resting on my chest, hoping it would make me invisible.

Mum and Dad arrived within minutes. I remember that they couldn't look me in the eye and I recall hearing profuse apologies – 'So sorry, Mr Shah, it will never happen again, we'll make sure of it, we're so terribly sorry . . . ' –

before I was made to stutter 'Sorry' too, and then Dad grasped my hand and marched me home. I sobbed all the way. I wasn't allowed any sweets for a month and my independent outings were curtailed for several more. But the look of disappointment on my parents' faces, the sense that I'd failed them, that was worse than any punishment.

I didn't set off that day intending to shoplift. It wasn't something I'd even imagined doing before. I thought people stole because they needed to, or because they were bad people, not because they felt like it. I would have perfectly happy with the amount of sweets I could afford, just as I had been every other Sunday. And there was no reason why I couldn't have chosen the Wispa bar, instead of the caramel bar or the other items I selected and paid for. Thinking about it now, if I'd really wanted that Wispa bar as well, and didn't have the money for it, Mr Shah would probably have let me have it. I could have dropped the money in another day.

So why did I do it? Good question. And why was it another six years before I did it again?

Posted by Robyn Hood at 3:05 PM
Comments: 0
Followers: 1
Blog Archive
Links

Chapter 10

'Excuse me, miss . . . '

It was almost bound to happen sooner or later, and Ruby knew that, but she'd never truly believed it would happen to her. She had taken the shoplifting statistics she'd read somewhere on the web too literally, because they made her feel more secure. Some boffin had sat down with a calculator and worked out that a shoplifter only gets caught once in forty-eight trips. But that didn't mean that Ruby could go out shoplifting forty-seven times and get away scot-free. She might have got caught the very first time she did it, or it could have happened on the seventh, tenth or one-hundredth trip. Then again, if she'd been really, really lucky, it might never have happened to her at all.

There had been a few near-misses, notably the time Noah had rescued her in Kelly's, and as a result she had become overconfident, too reliant on the belief that fate would always step in and pull her out of trouble at the last moment. The truth was, the nearer Ruby came to getting caught, the greater the thrill of her shoplifting expeditions. The more she shoplifted, the easier it seemed to her and the feeling that she'd got away with it yet again gave the experience an extra frisson of excitement, making the high she craved that little bit more intense. Half-consciously, she had started to take greater risks, choosing shops where the security was tighter, or where she looked conspicuous. And that was her downfall on the day she did get caught, at Zenda, an upmarket shop that sold designer labels and own brand clothes to young businesswomen who wanted to look both smart and fashionable.

The instant she walked into the store, the security guard clocked her. She was very obviously too young and too fresh-faced to be a businesswoman with a platinum credit card and a taste for well-cut suits. And she was either extremely stupid, or careless, or reckless – he couldn't decide which – because her coat was undone, revealing the local school's uniform. He recognised it because his elder daughter had gone there, a few years ago. Years of experience had taught him there were only two reasons why girls in school uniform came into Zenda. Either they were dragged there by their mothers, or they were there to shoplift. This girl was alone.

He decided to follow her around the store and watched as she flitted from aisle to aisle, sizing up the clothes, picking some of them up by their hangers and, it appeared at first glance, examining the fabric. He knew exactly what she was really doing; she was looking at the security tags, working out what type they were, and how easily they would come away. He sighed, sorry to be proved right. Then, with the absolute cynicism of someone who has seen it all a thousand times before, he bided his time, certain that a crime was about to be committed. He radioed his colleague and asked him to go to the exit doors, so they could block the teenage shoplifter's escape.

Across the aisle, he watched as the girl took a silky green blouse off its hanger and placed it on top of another identical blouse, doing it up so you could only see one garment. She repeated this process a few minutes later, covering a red, floral blouse with its identical twin. Then he tracked her as she walked around the shop, picking up jackets and trousers, as though she was trying to put an outfit together. He lost sight of her when she went into the changing room, but he knew exactly what would be happening behind the curtains of her cubicle. She would be removing the doubled-up blouses from their partners, pulling off their tags and hiding them in her bag, or wearing them under her own clothes. When she left the changing room it would appear that she had brought out the same number of garments as she had taken in; only she – and now he – would know any different.

She wasn't in the changing room for long, certainly not long enough to try on all the clothes she'd taken in with her. As she left, he radioed his colleague again, and he followed close behind her. He could tell she wasn't aware of him; she was probably focusing on making it out on to the street as fast as she could. 'Suspect approaching exit,' he radioed. 'Young girl, long hair, navy school uniform, over.'

'I see her,' came the reply. 'Over.'

He kept his distance as the electric doors parted for the girl and she stepped on to the pavement outside. He watched as she paused for a moment, possibly deciding whether to go left or right, and took his opportunity. 'Gotcha!' he said to himself. He made eye contact with his colleague and they surrounded Ruby, making it impossible for her to go anywhere but back into the shop.

'Excuse me, miss,' he said. 'We have reason to believe you have some items on your person that haven't been paid for.' He gently placed his hand on her shoulder, so there was no way he could later be accused of assault. You could never be too careful. 'Would you please open your bag?'

The look she gave him, her eyes wide with shock and fear, made him think momentarily of his daughter. But it wouldn't do to feel sorry for her. She was just another shoplifter, and he'd done his job.

Chapter 11

Ruby froze. She felt as if her legs were made out of lead and her insides were plummeting towards the floor. When she tried to speak, nothing came out. She let the security guard unzip her bag and rummage around inside, while she stood absolutely still. It didn't take him long to find and pull out the two blouses she had stolen. She watched as he held them up in the air like trophies, a smug look on his face. And then the plummeting sensation was gone, and it all came pouring out of her: streams of tears and snot, and loud, uncontrollable sobs. She could barely breathe. She was shocked at how upset she felt, and how scared, glad that no one she knew was around to witness what a crybaby she was. She really couldn't help herself. The guard handed her a tissue, without saying anything. He now looked as though he felt sorry for her; when he wasn't at work he was probably just someone's dad.

When Ruby had stopped crying quite so violently, the guard led her through a door at the back of the store, down a long corridor, past rooms that she had no idea existed. Some of them were full of clothes and boxes, others looked like offices. There was even a little kitchen area and a toilet. A few metres along, he stopped and knocked on a door, and then someone came out of one of the offices to meet them. She was a tall woman, with blond, curly hair and thin lips, and she was wearing one of the outfits Ruby had seen in the shop window. It didn't look as good on her as on the mannequin.

'I'm Lisa Farnworth, the manager,' she said, coldly. She looked Ruby up and down, taking in her school uniform and her bag and the streaks of mascara on her cheeks. 'Follow me.' She led Ruby, with the security guard walking behind, into another office at the end of the corridor, and shut the door behind them.

The office was dark and cold and it had no windows on to the street. There was nothing but a desk, two chairs and a filing cabinet. It felt like a prison cell, or, at least, what Ruby assumed a prison cell would be like; she'd never seen one except on TV. Maybe that was the point, maybe it was meant to scare her – a taste of things to come if she didn't reform. Ruby sat as she was instructed to do, sobbing quietly to herself, while the shop manager talked to the security guard, once breaking off to make a phone call. The discussion seemed to go on for hours. As hard as she strained her ears, Ruby couldn't make out what they were saying about her. Certain words rang out: 'young', 'amateur', 'attention', but without the other words in between they were meaningless. Ruby felt sick, as though she was waiting to be executed. She wondered if this was how Anne Boleyn had felt before she had her head chopped off. She'd always liked Anne best out of Henry VIII's wives; she sounded like she'd have been a good laugh, before she lost her head, that is.

The discussion was over, at last. 'We've decided we're not going to call the police this time,' said the manager. 'But we would like to speak to one of your parents.'

Ruby let out another sob. That was almost worse than facing the police. For a split second, she was nine years old again, standing in the newsagent's, her whole being crushed under the weight of her parents' disapproval. She bowed her head. Through strands of hair she could see a long scratch on the desk in front of her. She guessed it had probably been made by some other poor shoplifter, someone else whose parents had been called to share in their humiliation.

'So could we have your parents' number, please?'

'They're divorced,' said Ruby, still staring at the desk. 'They don't live together.'

'Well, would you prefer us to call your mum or your dad?'

'Um . . . I don't know . . . ' Mum would be

devastated, Ruby thought. First she would apologise to the store in such a heartfelt fashion anyone would think she was the one who'd stolen from them. Then she would take Ruby home and they would sit in the car in stony silence all the way. At home, the tension would be unbearable. For days, Mum would appear to be on the verge of tears and she would find it impossible to relax and talk to Ruby, so they'd just have clipped conversations about putting out the rubbish and making sure the heating was turned off. Worse, there would be long, whispered phonecalls, in which Mum and Dad would blame each other for Ruby's problem and discuss what they should do about her. There would be more arguments, and they might even decide to take her out of school and send her to the private school Dad preferred, after all. Without any notice. Right now, in the middle of her GCSEs. It didn't bear thinking about.

If, on the other hand, they called Dad, he would be shocked and angry at first, but once he saw Ruby's tears he would melt for sure, and he would soon forgive her. She'd tell him how stupid she had been and blame peer pressure and exam worries, and he would promise not to tell Mum and swear to sort it all out by himself. He would probably even enjoy keeping it secret from Mum.

'Well?' said the manager, impatiently.

'My dad,' muttered Ruby. 'But can I speak to him first, please?'

The manager nodded.

Ruby knew her dad's number was on her speed dial, but her brain was foggy and she couldn't remember whether it was at position three or four. Instead, fumbling, she scrolled through her address book and found his entry. She felt sick as she dialled, and relieved when the voicemail clicked in. She hesitated before putting the phone down, leaving him a few seconds of breathy silence. If he asked, she could always pretend she'd called him by accident; her phone was always doing that in her bag. Now what?

'Erm, straight to message,' she explained. 'Can I try another number for him?' She was lying. She didn't have another number (in truth, she did, but Dad was never at his house, so it wasn't even worth trying him on that), but she did have an idea that could potentially get her out of this mess without consequence.

She called the number. It rang four times, five times. Please pick up, she thought. Please be at home. Please don't let anyone else answer.

Chapter 12

'Hello,' said Noah.

'Hi, *Dad*.'

Noah was momentarily bewildered. It sounded like Ruby's voice, but why was she calling his house? And why was she calling him Dad? Had she dialled the wrong number? Thinking about it, the way she'd said 'Dad' was weird, as if she was trying to convey a secret message.

'I'm in a bit of trouble in a shop and there's someone who wants to talk to you.'

He heard her sniff. Had she been crying? 'Oh right, er . . . oh God, are you OK?' he said, perplexed and concerned. 'Um, do they, will they, um . . . you want me to . . . OK.' He felt his heart rate increase rapidly as he understood what she wanted him to do for her. Could he pull this off? He tried to remember how his dad sounded when he was talking to someone official about something important. If he could mimic his tone, the shape of his mouth, his expression, he might be able to do it.

'Mr Collins?' There was a strange woman's voice on the line now. Stern and a bit scary.

'Yes, this is Mr Collins. James Collins,' he said, in as low a baritone as he could muster. His voice came out so deep and so croaky that he sounded like one of those old Mafia bosses in gangster films. 'What seems to be the problem?'

'I'm Lisa Farnworth, the manager of Zenda clothes store. We have your daughter Ruby here. I'm afraid to tell you she's been caught shoplifting.'

Oh shit, thought Noah, she's gone and got herself caught. He felt angry with Ruby and scared for her, but also not all that surprised. He checked himself. How would a dad react? Would he be shocked? Or would he try to keep calm and in control? Noah was clueless. 'I see,' he said, gravely. 'That's terrible. I'm appalled. Her ... I've taught her better than that. She's never done anything like this before. I must apologise. What exactly did she take?' He cringed at his question. He wanted to know, but would that really be important to her dad? At this point?

The shop manager didn't appear to think it was an odd question. 'One of our security guards followed her from the store and found that she'd hidden two blouses in her bag. She had also removed the tags from said items. I'm afraid there's no doubt that she intended to steal them.'

'I see,' said Noah. 'And have the police been called?'

'Not yet, sir. Given that your daughter is a minor and that we believe this to be her first such offence, we thought we would speak to you and leave it to you to punish her in a way you see fit. She will, of course, be banned from all our stores for a period of a year. And we will expect payment for the goods, as they are no longer in sellable condition . . .'

Noah sighed. Stupid, stupid Ruby, he thought. He'd never heard of Zenda and couldn't picture what she might have stolen, or estimate how much it had cost. Girls' shops, their shopping habits and and their clothes were a mystery to him. He owned two pairs of trousers, some jeans, a few tops and a coat (plus his school uniform), and that was plenty. He only had one body to dress, after all. He couldn't understand why girls wanted new clothes every week, why they loved wasting hours trying them on and swapping them with their friends.

' . . . I hope she realises just how lucky she is,' the woman was saying. 'And that she's learned her lesson.'

'Oh yes, Ms Farnworth. I'm sure she has.' Noah hoped the conversation wouldn't continue for much longer. He couldn't maintain the croak; soon he'd have no voice left at all.

'So if we could just have the payment, please. It's a total of one hundred and sixty-nine pounds and ninety-eight pence.'

Noah gulped. For two blouses? What were they

made out of, gold? He didn't have instant access to that kind of money. He probably had that much in his savings account, but you had to give notice to get it out, and he couldn't do it without his parents' permission.

'So how would you like to pay? We can take a credit card, or you could come in and give us the cash when you pick your daughter up.'

The second option was clearly not viable. But neither was the first. He didn't have a credit card – he was fifteen years old. He started to panic. If he let Ruby down now he would be getting her, not to mention himself, into even more trouble. The police would probably be called after all. He had to think of something.

'Hold on a minute,' he said, hoping that the manager couldn't hear the fear in his voice. It was surely now a whole octave higher than before. There was a way he could pay, a credit card he could access, but he'd never intended to use it. He went over to his computer and typed in a series of passwords. 'Yes, it's, er . . . ' He read out the credit card number, the expiry date and then the three-digit security code. He felt nauseous. He'd never done anything like this before, and he was half expecting it not to work.

'Thank you, Mr Collins,' said the manager a few moments later. 'Are you going to come and fetch your daughter now?'

'Er, no, er, I'm at work, I'm afraid. We only live around the corner. She'll be fine to come home on her own.'

'Are you sure, Mr Collins?'

'Yes, thank you.'

'I'd feel happier if you came to pick her up, and if we could talk to you face to face. She is rather distressed.'

'It's not possible,' Noah said, in the strong voice his father used when he was telling his sisters that they couldn't have a bigger monthly allowance. It was a voice that said: this is the end of the matter.

'OK, Mr Collins, I trust we won't ever have reason to speak to you again.'

Me too, thought Noah. 'Yes, goodbye.'

He wanted the manager to put Ruby back on the phone so he could say, 'Phew, that was close,' and ask her exactly what had happened and tell her what he thought, but he knew that couldn't happen. He'd have to wait until later to get the lowdown from her. He sighed, hung up the phone, and turned back to his computer. The evidence of what he'd done to help Ruby beamed blatantly at him from the screen. Now they were both criminals. He closed the page down quickly and loaded up a computer game.

Chapter 13

The manager turned to Ruby. 'You're free to go now,' she said, with an expression that looked like pity. Poor girl, it seemed to say, her parents clearly don't care about her much; no wonder she's a thief. It made Ruby feel guilty. 'Free to go on condition that you do not return to this store, or any other branch for a year.'

'I promise,' said Ruby, rubbing her eyes dry with her knuckles, as she got up from her chair. She wondered if they were going to circulate *Wanted* posters of her around the country, to alert the other security guards and shop staff. *Ruby Collins: Wanted Dead or Alive.* Otherwise, how would they be able to stop her? What if she came in disguise? Not that she wanted to come into this shop ever again anyway. Overpriced rubbish. If the blouses had been better made they wouldn't have torn so badly when she pulled the security tags off, would they?

The manager showed Ruby to the door and asked the security guard to escort her from the premises. Ruby didn't know what to say, so she said, 'Thank you,' which felt wrong, but would have to do. She almost held out her hand so that manager could shake it, but that would have been weirder still. The security guard walked behind her until she was out on the street, then nodded, turned away and went back into the shop without saying anything.

Ruby had never felt so pleased to be outside. She didn't feel upset any more, just empty and a bit numb, as if all that crying had used up her emotions. She drank the air into her lungs, silently thanking Noah for helping her get away with it. She couldn't believe the telephone trick had worked. Noah's voice might have been deeper than most boys his age (frankly, some of them sounded like they'd been inhaling helium), but he didn't speak like a middle-aged man, not like her dad, anyway. Maybe it was different on the phone, a bit distorted, or maybe the shop manager had just wanted her money and the problem sorted quickly, and so hadn't wanted to ask too many questions.

That was another thing: Ruby couldn't believe that Noah had had to pay for the things she'd stolen, especially since it had been made very clear to her that she wouldn't be taking them home with her. How had

Noah been able to pay? How come he had a credit card?

She felt guilty; she wouldn't have asked him to help if she'd known he'd be made to pay. Somehow, she would have to find a way to pay him back. Maybe she could get a Saturday job, if her parents would let her. Her dad always said, 'If you need money, I'll give it to you. I don't want you working for minimum wage when you could be doing your coursework.' He didn't understand that she'd quite like to earn her own money, because it would make her feel more grown-up, more independent.

She decided to go straight round to Noah's to thank him, before she lost her nerve. Her mother would be expecting her home, wondering why she was so late back from school, but if she texted her to say where she was, it shouldn't be a problem. Mum would probably be pleased; she liked Noah. She'd never met Ross, but he wasn't the type of boy you introduced your mum to. Not that he'd have wanted to meet her anyway.

Going 2 C Noah xx, she texted, as she turned into her street. She took a small compact out of her bag and studied her face close up in the mirror. Her eyes were a bit puffy and her nose was red, but she didn't look too bad, considering. She toned down the redness with some powder, and smoothed her hair with her hand. It didn't occur to her to question why she cared what she looked like for Noah; she never had before. She wondered if he could see her coming from his usual vantage point at his bedroom window. But when she looked up there was no sign of him. Please be home, she thought. She rang the doorbell and waited. Please be home, she repeated to herself. A tall silhouette loomed up through the frosted glass and then, to her relief, Noah peered around the front door.

Chapter 14

Noah knew he shouldn't have been excited to see Ruby, but he couldn't help himself. His heart started racing whenever she was nearby. 'Hi,' he said brightly, as though he couldn't believe his luck. Then he reminded himself of what she'd made him do and how he should really be annoyed with her, and he tried to appear more serious. He cleared his throat. 'Hello.'

'Hi, Noah,' said Ruby. She was sheepish. 'I wanted to come round and thank you. I'm totally sorry about what happened. I mean it. You saved my life again!'

'You'd better come in,' he said, trying not to smile too broadly. He opened the door for her. She hadn't been in his house for years and he could see her eyes darting around, taking everything in. The hall would still have looked the way she recalled it, with the same colour paint and all the same pictures and hooks and mirrors.

'Your house smells just like I remember,' she commented. 'Nice, like lots of different perfumes all mixed up together.'

He shrugged. 'Course. That's because of all my sisters.'

'Poor Noah,' she teased. 'At least you're not an only child though. Believe me, it sucks.'

He nodded. 'Do you want to come up to my room?' he asked tentatively. 'My sisters are all home. I mean, we can talk better there.'

'Sure,' she said. She followed him up the stairs and into his bedroom. He sat down on his bed and was hoping she'd join him, but she sat in his office chair instead. She swivelled around in it, checking out his bedroom, just as she had the hall. He knew she'd be surprised at how bare it was. All the toys were gone, the walls were now plain white, and he'd taken down all his old posters. There was just a bookshelf, a desk, a wardrobe and the bed, which was covered in a duvet with a black and white geometric pattern.

'Where's all your stuff gone?' she asked.

'It's been tidied away' he said. 'And thrown away, some of it. It helps me think, not having too much clutter.'

'Oh,' she said. She laughed. 'I wouldn't know! My room is such a mess. Yours looks very grown-up.'

He shrugged, although he was pleased she'd said it.

He liked being thought of as grown up, especially by Ruby. 'So . . . ' he said, unsure how to steer the conversation back to what had happened earlier.

'So . . . ' she said. She giggled, nervously.

'What happened before? You nearly gave me a heart attack.'

'I don't really know,' said Ruby, quietly. 'Sorry.' She told him the whole story and he listened without interrupting. As she described how she felt when she'd been caught, she looked like she was going to cry again, and it made him want to hug her.

'It's OK,' he said. 'I'm not angry with you.'

She sniffed. 'Really?'

'Well, maybe a bit.'

She smiled. 'I need to ask you, how did you pay? How come you've got a credit card?'

'It doesn't matter,' he said. 'In fact, it's probably better if you don't know.'

'Oh,' she said, surprised. Thankfully, she didn't ask any other questions. 'Look, I promise I'm going to pay you back. Every last penny. I promise.'

'You don't have to,' he said. 'Really.'

'I will, honestly.'

He took a deep breath. 'I'd rather you just stopped stealing, Rubes.' He'd never called her that before; it just slipped out. It was what her dad used to call her, and saying it felt good. And maybe he'd now earned the right to be close to her, because she smiled. He added, 'I don't want you to get into big trouble.'

'I know,' she said. 'And I'm going to try. I promise. Honestly.'

He could never have predicted – or dreamed of – what happened next. Without another word, Ruby got up from her chair and walked over to him. Then she put her hands on his shoulders and she kissed him. She kissed him! It was far better even than he had imagined, her lips so much softer and sweeter. She pulled back, much too soon.

'I should go,' she said. She looked embarrassed.

Noah wasn't embarrassed. He was beaming, his eyes big and round. He had never felt so happy in his life. 'No, don't,' he said. All he knew was that he wanted to kiss her again. He pulled her gently on to his lap and put his arms around her waist, drawing her towards him. He didn't feel awkward or gangly or alone any more. If I'd have known this was going to happen, he thought, I'd have paid five thousand pounds to save her. Or five million.

Chapter 15

At the moment she said it, Ruby really did mean that she would try to stop shoplifting. She meant it with all her heart. And she still meant it when she awoke the next morning and, with a coy smile, remembered kissing Noah. She wasn't sure what had possessed her, but she knew she didn't regret it for a second. It hadn't been like kissing Ross, who was all tongue and wandering hands; it was gentle and slow and thrilling. She had felt as if she was falling, and yet at the same time she was perfectly safe. It was the weirdest feeling she'd ever experienced.

She was still adamant she wasn't ever going to shoplift again when she came straight home from school that Wednesday afternoon, without venturing anywhere near the high street. She was absolutely determined to stop. Had fate not stepped in, then perhaps her life, and

Noah's, would have taken a very different path. Who knows, maybe they would even have lived happily ever after together in their cul-de-sac.

It wasn't to be, for bigger, unseen forces were at work. Unknowingly, by writing her blog, by being in 'the right place at the right time', Ruby had tapped into the zeitgeist – an invisible 'feeling' in the air when, all of a sudden, almost everybody is thinking the same things and talking about the same things, and no one knows why, or how, or where it all started.

First, a report was published by the Government revealing that there had been a massive increase in shoplifting in Britain, particularly by young people. The report might only have made a brief appearance in the news, had it not been for another event. That month, a new film version of the story of Robin Hood was due to be released in cinemas. It starred several of Hollywood's biggest names and was directed by a multi-Oscar winning director, and it had cost hundreds of millions of dollars to make. There was so much money and so much publicity attached to the film, that unless you lived alone, in a cave, under the ground, in deepest Siberia, you couldn't have failed to hear about it. Even then, a nosy vole might burrow down to tell you. The film was like a giant snowball, rolling faster and faster, and growing larger and larger, scooping up everything in its path and taking it along for the ride. Its release also ensured that the topic of stealing – particularly the rise in shoplifting highlighted by the Government report – became *the* major talking point.

Ruby had no inkling that this giant snowball had rolled over her blog, making it a must-read for thousands of strangers. How could she? It probably happened a little like this: lots of people put the title of the new film into a search engine to find out more. What they found, in addition to all the movie publicity, was Ruby's blog. Noah's technical wizardry had served her well. When setting up her blog he had made sure that certain key words contained within it would be linked with millions of invisible pathways all over the internet. And so, every time somebody searched for the name 'Robin Hood' or even 'Robyn Hood' (if they couldn't spell or type well), or for 'stealing' or 'shoplifting', it would trigger one of these pathways, and create a direct link to Ruby's blog. Soon, tens, then hundreds, then thousands of people had stumbled across it. Many of them took no notice of it at all, but there were others who took the trouble to read her words, and some of them liked what they found. These people added Ruby's blog to their favourites, and some of them told their friends about it, who told their friends. Then there were others, who were shocked or horrified by what they read. They too told other people about the blog; a few of them even wrote about it in their own blogs. The more that it was read, the more prominent it became in the results of every search engine. Within days, Ruby's blog had a become a snowball of its own, picking up followers and detractors from across the web.

The first she knew of it was when she logged in to write a new entry, a week after she'd been caught at Zenda. It had taken her that long to calm down and process what had happened, and she hadn't even been sure that she wanted to blog again. It wasn't just having to face the humiliation of admitting in print that she'd been caught after all her bravado, it was the fact that unless she went out shoplifting again, she wouldn't have anything to write about. What, she thought, is the point of having a blog about shoplifting if you don't do it? It's like writing about who makes the juiciest burgers, and deciding to become a vegetarian. What changed her mind was the realisation that writing her blog calmed her; she could tell it things she couldn't tell her friends. If she wasn't going to go out shoplifting again, she needed this release more than ever. Her last entry had been her bravest to date: it not only detailed what she'd been up to, but also gave practical tips on how best to shoplift.

She logged on to see this, at the bottom of the entry:
Followers: 1633
Comments: 280
At first, she thought she had opened the wrong blog. Surely it must be a mistake? 1633 followers? As far as she knew, Noah was her blog's only follower, if not its only reader. But then she began to look at the comments and she knew, with certainty, that many, many people really had read her blog.

This blog epitomises everything that's wrong with society and young people today. Proud of yourself, are you, Robyn? You have no morals. Your parents should be ashamed of you. I'm disgusted.
Barbara Flowers, Kent

You're going to burn in hell Robyn Hood.
Godisgreat

Way 2 go Robyn! Share the wealth!
Old Socialist

I think you're making it all up. You don't even have the guts to reveal your real name.
Anonymous

You're deluded. Just because you're giving the things you steal to charity doesn't make it right. If you want to help a charity shop, go and volunteer at one.
Carol Miller

Where are the charity shops you take your stuff to? I wanna buy your gear.
Maid Marian

I've got a shoplifting tip for you: don't do it!
Mark, Runcorn

I'm sick of being ripped off by big stores too. They don't even miss the stuff shoplifters take – they're insured for it.
Anya, Romford

I work in a clothes shop and it's people like you who make my job a misery and keep the prices high. Get over yourself.
Lisa

I used to shoplift all the time and I never got caught. I only stopped because I got bored of doing it. Bet you will too one day.
Martina, Worcester

Hey Robyn, I want a brand new PlayStation. Any tips on how to steal one? Where's the best place to go?
Robin Banks

Some free advice for you: don't think that you can't get done before you leave the shop. They can do you for concealing something too, if they catch you putting it in your bag or coat. They argue you clearly intended to steal it. It's worth remembering this.
Natalie, Barnes

Charity begins at home, not at your local department store.
Megan

'Oh my God! Oh my God!' Ruby exclaimed, as she scrolled her way down. She was too excited to stay seated, so she jumped up and paced around her bedroom, in an attempt to burn off the adrenalin that was sparking through her body. Her arms and legs felt tingly and hot; she could barely control them. Who were all those people? How had they found her blog? Why were some of them saying such nasty things about her?

'Oh my God! Oh my God!' She needed to talk about it. To tell someone. Who could she call? Only Noah, of course. Had he seen the comments on her blog? Why hadn't he told her about them? Was he upset with her? Thank goodness she'd got his mobile number from him on the evening they'd kissed. She hadn't used it until now because she wasn't sure quite what she felt about him. They'd made no future plans when she'd left his house, and they hadn't bumped into each other in the street since, which she was glad about because she wasn't sure what she would have said. At school she'd kept out of his way, not exactly avoiding him, smiling and saying hello, but never stopping long enough to have a proper conversation.

She'd been thinking about him a great deal though, more than she had in years (which wasn't saying very much, given that she'd hardly thought of him at all since they were kids). All she knew was that she liked him and that she'd enjoyed kissing him, but beyond that, she didn't know what she wanted from him. He wasn't her boyfriend or even a proper friend, at least not in the way that her other friends were. It was difficult to see how that would change. What did they have in common, apart from her blog and the fact they lived in the same street? Yet he was such easy company, and being around him made her feel safe and calm – emotions which she rarely felt when she was with her other friends, or anybody else for that matter. It was because she didn't have to try with him; she could be herself and he accepted it. Nothing she did or said ever shocked or upset him, or made him stop liking her. He *got* her.

How, she wondered, was it possible that they were the same age, when he seemed so much older and wiser than her? Boys were supposed to be more immature, weren't they? That was why girls her age went out with boys Ross's age. But Noah made Ross look like a stupid kid. Ross *was* a stupid kid. If she was honest with herself, she much preferred Noah . . .

There was just too much to think about. Her brain was beginning to hurt. Before she could change her mind, she found Noah's number in her address book and pressed *Call*. She had butterflies in her tummy, which she thought weird, because calling Noah really shouldn't have made her nervous.

'Hey!' she said, when he picked up.

'Hey Ruby, how are you?' he said. He sounded flustered, and that made her feel jittery too.

'I'm OK,' she said breathlessly. 'Listen, have you seen my blog? It's all gone mental.'

'No,' he said. 'I haven't looked at it since . . . Not for a while, anyway. What's happened?'

'Just look!'

'OK, OK,' he said. 'I'm logging in now. Hang on a second . . . Wow! You have so many followers. Where did they all come from?'

'I don't have a clue! I thought you might know something.'

'Nothing to do with me, I promise,' he said. 'I haven't told anyone anything.' He was silent for a moment. 'Jeez, I've just read some of the comments! They're a bit full-on.'

'Yeah, I know,' Ruby said. 'A bit nasty and scary. They can't find out who I am or where I live, can they?'

'Course not,' said Noah. 'There's no way. I've got it all encrypted for you.'

'Phew,' she said, allowing herself to be reassured, even though she wasn't certain what encrypted meant. 'Thanks. Where did they all come from? I mean, why are they reading my blog?'

'I dunno. I can find out exactly for you if you like.'

'Yeah, how?'

'By . . . It's techie stuff. Don't think you want to know. Honestly.'

She giggled. 'I guess not.'

'It's probably key words. Thinking about it, that

Robin Hood film is about to come out, isn't it? Robin Hood stuff is everywhere.'

'I didn't think of that. So they all think my blog is something to do with the film?'

'Maybe. Hey, people could think it's some sort of viral marketing campaign. They must be really confused.'

'Yeah.' She laughed again. 'They're looking for Sherwood Forest and they get our local high street.' She paused for thought. 'God, Noah, it's weird knowing all those strangers have read what I wrote and are judging me. I think some of them really hate my guts.'

'They're just nutters. Ignore them. And look, some of them think you're great. Did you read this one? It's from someone called Charley. He cleared his throat. *I love your blog,* she says, *I shoplift too and you totally understand how I feel. I don't feel so alone now.*'

'Wow!' Ruby said. 'I didn't think I was actually helping people. That's cool.'

'Yeah, and this one . . . They don't give a name. *Stealing gives me a lift too. I know it's wrong, but I can't stop. I don't even want the stuff. Now I've read your blog, I'm going to take it all down to the charity shop tomorrow.*'

'I'm an inspiration!' said Ruby, in a self-mocking tone, although she was beaming inside. She liked having that much attention, even if nobody knew who she was. 'That's so weird. Oh my God.' She couldn't help grinning. 'So how are you, Noah?'

'I'm good,' he said. 'I'm fine. I haven't seen you

around much this week. What have you been up to?'

'Oh you know, this and that.'

'Right,' he said.

'But none of *that*,' she added. 'I really have been trying.'

'That's great,' he said. He sounded happy for her. 'I knew you could do it.' There was a silence. 'Uh, about the other night . . . I was hoping we'd bump into each other . . . '

Ruby felt her face glow hot. 'I know. I guess we've both been busy.'

'Yeah,' he said. 'Probably. I would have called you, but I realised you didn't give me your number when I gave you mine. I should have asked. Anyway, I've got it now . . . I was going to say . . . Listen, what are you up to?'

'You mean now?' she asked.

'Yeah. It's just, I don't know if you want to . . . I was wondering if . . . Do you want to come round?'

'I don't know. I mean, I was just about to write a blog entry,' she said, truthfully. To her surprise, going round to Noah's struck her as an appealing idea. She didn't want an excuse not to go. 'But it won't take long,' she added. 'Give me half an hour.'

It was strange writing for an audience, instead of only for herself. It made her self-conscious about which words she used and, for the first time, she felt she didn't know where to start. Conscious of the time, she decided just to bash something out. People would think whatever they wanted to think, anyway. They always do. Instead of what really happened at Zenda, she wrote what she imagined would have happened had that expedition been successful. It was a short piece of fiction, based partially on reality, a bit like doing her English language coursework. She wondered what her English teacher would think were she to hand in her blog one day. What a way to confess that would be! She felt a bit of a fraud for lying, but it was her blog and she could write whatever she wanted, couldn't she? If thousands of people were reading it now, it wouldn't be fair to disappoint them by admitting she'd been caught, that it had terrified her, and so she wasn't planning to shoplift again. But she didn't put in as much detail as usual, for fear of tripping herself up (and, more trivially, because she wanted to make sure she had time to redo her make-up before she went round to see Noah). When she'd finished, she felt satisfied and full of anticipation for the comments she might receive. Noah will understand why I've lied, she told herself. And isn't lying better than stealing?

He was very understanding, although the truth was they didn't do much talking. Somehow, within minutes of arriving at Noah's house, Ruby found herself kissing him again. Or maybe it was he who kissed her. Either way, this time Ruby couldn't make any excuses. While kissing someone once could be called an accident, doing it twice means you must really like them.

Robyn Hood's Blog

I steal from expensive stores and give to charity shops

March 24

I'm getting better at this. Better and bolder. The other day, I went into one of those really posh shops, the ones where everything is made of silk and leather and cashmere, and where all the customers have swishy, glossy hair with highlights, and perfect nails with matching lipstick, and I took two tops. One of them was a bright apple-green blouse with a pussy bow, and the other one was a wine-red coloured tunic, with purple and pink winter roses splattered all over it. They were both made from pure silk and were crazily expensive for tops, and I have no idea when anybody would wear them, but they felt so soft and so smooth, and they even smelled expensive, which would make you want them anyway. I knew I couldn't resist them, even though if I'd put either of them on I'd have looked like I was a kid who'd raided the dressing-up box.

I was in and out of the shop in ten minutes, the tops folded neatly in my bag. The tags weren't hard to get off; they were the type you can deactivate with a magnet. I decided to split them between two of my favourite charity shops, telling each of them the same story about how my mum had bought a top for a posh do, but had put on so much weight she couldn't wear it any more. Like all the best lies, it was almost true: Mum is always getting rid of clothes because she's put on weight. It's all those cakes and biscuits she bakes for everyone; she says she never eats them herself, but I've seen her scoffing the broken bits (she tells herself they don't count because they're not actual biscuits). Mum hates getting rid of her clothes. She'll keep them for a couple of years first, in the hopes that she'll get back into them, but she never does.

The charity shops were very grateful for 'Mum's weight gain' – the volunteer at the sick animals shop put the apple-green blouse straight on the mannequin in the window. She said she could probably sell it for fifteen quid. The tunic with roses on has been priced at twelve. Job done.

Posted by Robyn Hood at 9:32 PM
Comments: 351
Followers: 3200
Blog Archive
Links

Chapter 16

When Ruby woke up on Monday morning, she was a celebrity, although she didn't yet know it. Over the weekend, a national newspaper journalist had found out about the growing popularity of Robyn Hood's blog and written an article blaming young people like her for all society's ills. Maybe it was a good thing she didn't see it, because it called her 'morally vacant', 'deluded' and 'in serious need of discipline and education'. Within hours, almost a hundred thousand people had looked at her blog. By Monday, other papers had picked up on the story, and it had begun to be discussed on the radio and on TV. Ruby's mum, who had the day off work, actually heard one of the broadcasts as she made lunch, although she was, of course, totally oblivious to the fact that it was about her daughter, or that the blog in question was produced in the room directly above her head.

'And today, listeners, we're talking about shoplifting. A mystery teenage blogger who claims to steal from expensive stores and give her spoils to charity shops is generating furious debate. Do you think that she's a modern day Robin Hood? Is she deluded? Why, as a government report revealed last week, is shoplifting on the rise? Have you ever done it? Did you get caught? Call in now with your stories and views.'

Interesting, thought Pam Collins, only half-listening as she scraped butter across a slice of toast and planned her afternoon activities. She was going to have her hair done and she had a dentist's appointment, and she also needed to pop into the supermarket, and pay in a cheque.

Ruby's dad heard a similar radio phone-in show as he drove up the motorway to a conference. He had stopped off at a service station for a coffee and only tuned into the discussion halfway through.

'So what you're saying is that if you give what you've stolen to a good cause, it's OK?' said the presenter.

'Yeah, it's for charity, innit?' said a man with a deep voice.

'But surely being charitable means donating your own possessions, not those that belong to someone else? I'll remind you, the blogger who calls herself Robyn Hood is shoplifting and then giving the goods to charity shops to ease her own conscience.'

'Yeah,' said the man. *'It's cos it's all so expensive, right?'*

'*Right, er, thank you, Joe,*' said the presenter, abruptly ending the call.

Moron, thought James Collins.

'*Time for another caller. We've got Hazel from Kent on the line. Hazel, what do you think of Robyn Hood?*'

'*Shocking,*' said Hazel. '*In my day, teenagers didn't do things like that. They had respect. It wouldn't happen if they brought back National Service.*'

James sighed, reached over to his radio tuner and found a music station instead. He put his foot on the accelerator and didn't give the mystery blogger another thought all the way to Manchester.

As for Ruby, while her exploits were being discussed and her character dissected across the airwaves, she was at school, daydreaming about Noah. Every time she tried to make herself concentrate on what the teacher was saying, or attempted to read a paragraph of her history textbook, an image of his face would leap into her head, and she wouldn't be able to stop herself thinking about him. It was one of the weirdest feelings she'd ever experienced. Two weeks earlier, she would have sworn she wouldn't fancy Noah if he were the last guy on earth. Now, she couldn't imagine wanting anyone else, least of all Ross. She decided that kissing somebody for hours must produce some kind of chemical reaction which messes with your brain. Like a natural love potion. Why else would she have butterflies every time she thought of Noah? Why else would she be longing to kiss him again? She kept stealing glances at him across the corridor or in the playground, when she hoped he wasn't looking. Objectively, he was still far too lanky, with bad hair and rubbish clothes, but he had such lovely eyes, especially when he smiled, and such gorgeous thick lashes. She could gaze at them for hours. How could she not have noticed that before? How could her friends not have noticed it either?

At lunchtime, she, Amanda and Hanni sneaked out to Burger King. Only sixth formers were officially allowed off the school premises during school hours, but it was rare that anybody noticed, as long as you were back at class after lunch and didn't cause any trouble in the local shops. Ruby didn't feel very hungry, so she ordered a portion of fries and picked at them, while the others scoffed burgers.

'Ruby, hon, are you on a diet?' asked Amanda.

'Hardly, I'm eating fries!'

'I wouldn't call that eating. You have to put the food in your mouth, chew it and swallow it to make it count. I should know.' Amanda's older sister had suffered from anorexia, so she thought she was an expert on eating disorders and had the right to comment on her friends' calorie intake. She became anxious if anyone ordered a salad, or refused a piece of chocolate.

'Honestly, Mand, I'm just not hungry.'

Amanda fixed her with a critical stare. 'I'm a bit worried about you, Ru. You hardly ever want to come out these days. And you never hang out with Ross and the guys. He's a bit miffed.'

'If he was that bothered, he would call me,' said Ruby, irritated. 'Or hasn't he worked out how to use a phone yet?'

'Fair point,' said Amanda. 'I know you two aren't serious. But he is cute, I've always thought so. Are you sure you want to leave him hanging? I can't see him waiting around for you.'

Ruby shrugged. 'He's selfish and unreliable and vain. I'm fed up of him, Mand. You can have him if you like.'

'That's not what I meant! I don't want your cast-offs, thanks. Hey, what's up with you lately? You've been acting dead weird, staying in a lot, always going straight home from school. Are you OK? Hanni, has she said anything to you?'

Hanni shook her head and gave Ruby a sympathetic glance.

'Nothing's up, honest. I'm fine,' said Ruby. 'I've just had a load of coursework and family stuff, you know.'

'Yeah,' said Hanni. 'We know.'

Ruby took a deep breath. She didn't need to be a clairvoyant to guess what the answer would be before she asked the question, but she had to ask it anyway. 'So, what do you two think of Noah?'

'Noah the nerd?' said Hanni, raising her eyebrows.

Ruby nodded.

'Are you serious? What's there to think about?'

'I don't know . . . I just think he's a nice guy. There's more to him than you think. He's . . . Don't you think he's got lovely eyes?'

Amanda giggled loudly. 'She's lost it. Hanni, she's totally lost it! Ruby, sweetie, you're so out of his league! You can have guys like Ross, why on earth would you be interested in Noah? I doubt he's into girls, anyway. Just computers. And maybe trains.'

'It's not like that,' said Ruby, backtracking. Her friends were never going to accept Noah as potential boyfriend material, she realised. They couldn't even begin to look at him the way she did, as a guy, instead of a geek. 'I was just thinking aloud. You know, he's my neighbour, and he's helped me with my computer, and I just think he's got nice eyes. I don't mean anything by it.'

'That time you came to pick me up for school,' said Hanni, suspiciously. 'You were with him then. It's obvious he has a thing for you. Have you been *seeing* him?'

'Don't be ridiculous. He's just an old friend. We often bump into other in the street and have a chat. I do think he might have a bit of a crush on me though.' She laughed.

'Phew,' said Amanda. 'I was a bit worried about you there. I thought you had a serious bad taste issue.'

'Yeah,' said Hanni. 'Imagine kissing him. You'd need to stand on a step ladder.'

'And you might get burned by the sun!' Amanda spluttered.

'Don't be mean,' Ruby said, remembering with the flicker of a smile what it was really like to kiss Noah. She wanted to say, 'The truth is, kissing him is amazing, much nicer than kissing Ross – he's a real natural,' but she didn't want her friends to choke to death on their burgers. Instead, she half-heartedly joined in with their laughter at Noah's expense. It made her feel sad and conflicted. She might have decided she liked Noah, but what her friends thought was important too. She needed a boyfriend who would get on with them, whom they respected, who was someone they'd want to hang out with. Noah was none of those things. It didn't mean she couldn't see him, but maybe it was better if they kept their relationship a secret, for now at least. He'd understand, wouldn't he? He was already the keeper of her biggest secret, and he'd told her he liked being the only person who knew who she really was. Maybe, then, he'd enjoy having a secret relationship too. It was quite romantic, if you looked at it a certain way.

'So, are you going to dump Ross, then?' asked Amanda.

'Nah, I'll just leave things how they are. As in nowhere. We're not officially going out, never have been, so I don't officially need to dump him, do I?'

'True,' said Hanni. 'And he probably wouldn't take it very well, would he? He'd get all macho about it. It's best if you let him think he's dumped you.'

Ruby shrugged. She had zero interest in what Ross felt. 'If he wants.'

The man at the next table got up to go, leaving his newspaper behind, 'Hey,' said Amanda, reaching over to grab it. 'Look, Hanni, there's a story about Cheryl Cole here for you.'

'Ooh, let's see,' said Hanni. She skimmed the article, then pushed the paper away, nonplussed. 'That's not news. I already knew that weeks ago.'

'Give it here,' said Amanda. She went through a few pages, just glancing at the pictures and reading the headlines, until something caught her interest. 'Hey, you know we were going to see *Robin Hood* on Friday night, did you hear about this?' She turned the paper around so the others could see.

Robyn Hood, Princess of Thieves

An anonymous teenage blogger who calls herself Robyn Hood is causing a stir online. This gym-slip outlaw, who really does wear tights under her school uniform, BRAGS about shoplifting pricey gear from designer stores and then donating it to CHARITY shops. In her detailed internet diaries she BOASTS about the BUZZ she gets from stealing jewellery, nicking underwear, swiping silk tops and pilfering knitwear. She even gives readers TIPS on how to shoplift themselves . . .

'Yeah,' said Hanni. 'I heard about it on the radio before I went to school.'

'What a muppet!' Amanda said. 'Why go to the trouble of stealing stuff if you're not going to keep it?'

'For the buzz I think.' Hanni chewed her lip. 'But then she feels guilty and wants to get rid of it. Sort of makes sense.'

Ruby put down her fries. Acid was rising in her throat and she felt as if she was about to throw up. 'I don't feel very well,' she mumbled, scrambling out of her seat as quickly as she could. The toilets were on the other side of the restaurant and she didn't know if she would make it. She was lightheaded and her heart was beating so fast it felt as if it was going to explode from her chest. Retching, she managed to find her way inside a cubicle just in time. Afterwards, she sat on the closed toilet seat for a few minutes, her head between her knees, breathing as slowly and deeply as she could. None of her thoughts were coherent.

'Are you all right in there?' It was Hanni's voice. 'We're worried about you.'

'I'm OK,' Ruby said, shakily. 'I'll be out in a minute. Go back to the table.'

When she was sure Hanni had left, she opened the cubicle door and went to the sink to wash her hands and her face. Her legs felt as if they wouldn't carry her and she had to lean against the sink for support. The fluorescent lighting above the mirror did her no favours. There she was, *the* Robyn Hood, and she looked terrible, her skin pale and blotchy.

When she came back to the table, both her friends peered at her with concern.

'God, Ru, you look so white. What's wrong?' said Amanda.

'I don't know. I must have eaten something dodgy for breakfast.'

Hanni put her hand on Ruby's arm. 'I think you should go home. We'll cover for you.'

'Thanks,' Ruby said. She wanted to be alone, to have time to think. Now the shock was wearing off she no longer felt nauseous, but her head was beginning to throb. She picked up her coat and her bag. 'I think I'll go now, if that's OK.'

'Course it is. We'll call you later,' said Amanda.

'Look after yourself,' said Hanni.

Ruby walked home slowly and cautiously, as if she was no longer sure that the paving stones would bear her weight without cracking. It was a journey she had made every day for years, and yet everything seemed different, shifted, slightly out of focus perhaps – she couldn't put her finger on what had changed. She bowed her head, afraid to make eye contact with anybody who passed by. What if they were someone who had read her blog or gossiped about her? What if they could tell that she was Robyn Hood?

It still seemed incredible to her that she'd had no inkling of what had been going on around her. Weren't your ears supposed to burn if people talked about you?

How could she not have realised that *tens of thousands of people* were discussing her actions and her private thoughts, criticising her, hating her even? Tens of thousands of people. It was one thing seeing a few hundred comments on her blog – and that had been enough of a shock – quite another knowing that she was being written about in the papers and picked apart on the radio.

By the time she reached her front door, her mood had transformed. The shock was fading and, instead, she was beginning to think about what being famous could mean. She was growing excited, euphoric even. Wasn't this what she'd always wanted? To be someone? To be talked about? To be a celebrity? To make a mark? She went straight into her bedroom and switched on her computer. What else had been written about her? She had googled her name a few times, like everyone had, but, aside from her Facebook page, she had only ever found two mentions of Ruby Collins, both related to her school netball team. Googling Robyn Hood brought up so many hits she didn't know where to start looking. Instead, she decided to do a newspaper search. She'd never looked at the newspapers online in her life, but now she had the urge to read every one. Several of them had stories about her, and one of them, the boring one that Mum brought home with her from work sometimes, even had comments from the Archbishop of Canterbury! Apparently, the reason she – and people like her – shoplifted was because of the breakdown of society and the destruction of local communities. Ruby didn't really understand what he meant but she was fairly certain that wasn't what motivated her. Funny, she thought, if only he'd asked me I'd have told him I did it because sometimes I feel bored and frustrated. Hasn't he read my blog? For a second, Ruby flirted with the idea of sending the Archbishop a letter telling him he didn't know what he was talking about, but she had no idea where to send it. What was his address? Archbishop of Canterbury, Canterbury? And what should she call him? Dear Sir? Dear Archie?

Her thoughts started to run away with her. Maybe she'd be invited to the premiere of the Robin Hood film next week. Maybe she'd do the chat-show circuit. The hosts would love her, and whatever bands were on their shows that week would hear her singing to herself in the green room and ask her to sing live with them. A single would be sure to follow. Maybe she'd be able to start hanging out with Lily Allen and Robert Pattinson and Brangelina. This was far better than going out shoplifting. The buzz was so much bigger, so much more intense . . .

And then it struck her. If she wanted this to continue, she would have to give people – give her *fans* – what they wanted. And what they wanted was more of Robyn Hood's blog. What they wanted was for her to engage them with exciting tales of her dangerous exploits, to shock them and surprise them and anger them. If the blog was going to maintain their interest, Robyn would have to take greater risks and steal more expensive things. She certainly couldn't get caught.

Ruby sighed. She would just have to make it up. She leant back in her chair, opened up her blog and began to write a new entry.

Chapter 17

Noah felt uncomfortable reading Ruby's latest blog. It was all rubbish, of course, all a fantasy. At the time she claimed to have been out shoplifting she had actually been with him. Still, it was better that she was making things up than stealing again, and risking getting caught. In the blog, she said she'd visited the designer floor of the local department store and stolen a crimson dress worth five hundred pounds from under the noses of two shop assistants and a security guard. Five hundred pounds, he thought, you could get a second-hand car for that, or a holiday! Brazenly, she said she'd worn it home, under her own clothes. She said it looked too pristine to be second-hand, so she'd roughed it up a little bit, dulling its sheen and creating a few loose threads. Then, she said, she'd gone back to the high street and dropped it off at the sick animals charity shop, telling them that it had been her school prom dress and she'd never have another occasion to wear it, so she wanted it to go to a good cause.

He was impressed by the way Ruby had described the dress. She'd used all kinds of tempting words, like luscious and silky, which made it sound like something anyone would want. Any girl, obviously. He was sure his sisters would have killed each other for it. If it had existed. Later, Ruby would tell him that she'd found a dress on an internet shopping site and copied its description, adding a few extra, imaginative details of her own. It was a make she knew the department store sold, so there was no reason the dress couldn't have been shoplifted from there, no reason at all why people would doubt her tale.

Noah wasn't so sure. Even if he hadn't known the truth, it was obvious to him that the whole story was made up because its tone was completely different from her earlier, genuine blog entries. Ruby's true accounts were honest and thoughtful. This was just boastful, with no hint of the fear or guilt that he knew she felt when she went out shoplifting. He wasn't sure he liked Robyn Hood; he'd never have fallen for her.

Just a few days before, he would have said life was as close to perfect as anything not designed like a microchip could be. Ruby had admitted that she liked him too – in actions rather than words – but they count more, don't they? Not only that, but she had stopped stealing – or so she'd said, and he was inclined to believe her, in spite of what she had written in her blog – and he had really thought he'd now have a shot at being her boyfriend. Finally, after all these months of daring to dream about it. He'd have settled for her friendship, if that was all that was on offer, but she'd wanted more. It hadn't seemed real or possible until he said the words out loud, so he'd confided in his eldest sister (leaving out the shoplifting parts of the story, and obviously not going into any detail about the kissing bit), and she was thrilled for him. She didn't even tease him about it much, although there was more hair patting than usual, and whenever she saw him she'd grin broadly and wink.

But now Ruby's blog had taken on a life of its own and he had a gnawing feeling in his gut that the attention it was receiving would draw her away from him. When he'd spoken to her, a few hours earlier, she had been so excitable and breathless he could barely make out what she was saying. She kept going on about being famous and how weird it all was, and asking him if he'd read the stories about her blog in the papers, or heard anything about it on the radio or TV. After her call he'd spent a good hour going through the articles and comments on the web and they had only made him feel anxious and irritable. All those people talking about Ruby – or rather, Robyn – knew nothing about her. Not like he did. They were just speculating about her, judging her, jumping to conclusions. He wanted Ruby to himself for a while, not in a creepy way, but so he could spend some proper time with her. He'd waited long enough! He certainly didn't want to share her with a load of strangers. Why Ruby even wanted to be famous made no sense to him. He couldn't think of anything worse than being followed, having people crawling all over your life, trying to burrow their way in, like those insects that lay eggs under your skin.

Thinking about it all made him feel angry but he couldn't articulate why, or say exactly where, or at whom his anger was directed. He had a feeling of helplessness, of being out of control. It made him want to hit something, but he wasn't a violent person, so he took his rage out on a computer game instead. That didn't help; he was too angry to concentrate and so his score was pitiful, which made him feel even angrier and more frustrated than ever. It occurred to him to take Ruby's blog down, to make it disappear forever, so that everybody would go away and leave him alone with her, but he knew that wouldn't be fair or right and, most of all, it would just make her hate him.

He thought he might feel better if he talked to her about it all, so he decided to pop round to see her after dinner. In retrospect, perhaps he was stupid just to turn up at her front door and ring the bell. Maybe he should have thought to text or call first. But he didn't stop to think.

Her mum let him in. She was friendly and acted like he was expected. All she said was, 'Hello Noah. Nice to see you. Ruby's upstairs, in her room,' and motioned for him to go up. He wondered if she knew about him and Ruby but if she did, she didn't give anything away. The thought of seeing Ruby close up again, instead of across a classroom or in a corridor, made him feel excited and nervous, which made him clumsy, and he tripped himself up on the stairs. He was glad she didn't see that. Her bedroom door was shut and he stood outside for a few moments, composing himself and catching his breath. Then he knocked on her door. There was no answer. He knocked again. Still no answer. He didn't know what to do. Should he go in? What if she wasn't dressed? He had to delete *that* image from his mind. He hung back for a while, before knocking one last time.

'What is it Mum?' he heard Ruby shout. 'Come in!'

Tentatively, he pushed the door open, craning his neck around it. 'Hi Rubes, it's, er, not your mum, it's me.' The room was lit only by a table lamp, but he could just make out Ruby's shape in the far corner. She was sitting on the floor on some cushions and there appeared to be two other figures crouched next to her.

'God, Noah! Um, er, come in,' she said, hesitantly. 'We're just watching a DVD.'

He stepped into the room. In the glow of the lamp he could see three pairs of eyes peering up at him.

'All right, Noah,' said Amanda, with the hint of a

smirk in her voice.

'Oh, hi, Noah,' said Hanni. She didn't sound too pleased to see him either.

He was hoping that Ruby would get up to greet him, but she didn't move from the cushions. When he got closer he could see that she and Hanni were squashed up together on a single beanbag. That must be why she hadn't moved. So he leant down towards Ruby, to kiss her hello.

'Um, er, what are you doing?' she said abruptly, moving her head away from him.

Amanda and Hanni sniggered behind their hands.

'I was . . . I was just saying hello,' he said. It was only going to be a kiss on the cheek. He felt sick with humiliation, glad that the darkness meant nobody would see how embarrassment had stained his face and neck beetroot red.

'Oh right, yes, sorry.' She seemed nervous, awkward, guilty. It was clear she hadn't told her friends about him, that she was ashamed of their relationship. 'Er, this is Noah from across the road. You know Hanni and Amanda. From school. They came to see if I was OK. I had to go home early because I wasn't feeling well.'

She knew that he already knew all this. Why was she acting as if he was a stranger? With every word she spoke he felt as if he was being stuck with a knife.

'Are you all right?' she asked. He wasn't sure if it was a pleasantry, or if she was genuinely concerned about how he might be feeling after her brush off. When she was sure her friends couldn't see, she shook her head gently, mouthing the word 'sorry' to him, and then 'later'.

'I'm fine,' he said, flatly. 'And you?'

'Good,' she said. 'Much better, thanks.' There was a painful silence. 'Did you want something? I mean, did you come over for a reason?'

Hanni and Amanda shuffled on their cushions, uncomfortably.

What was he supposed to say? *Yes, I came to see you because I thought you were my sort-of girlfriend?* 'Um, yes . . . ' He was lucky he could think quickly. He put his hand in the back pocket of his jeans, where he kept his memory stick, and pulled it out. 'I just brought over that software you wanted. I was going to install it for you.'

'Thanks, Noah,' said Ruby. 'That's really very sweet of you, but could we do it later, or tomorrow, when my friends aren't here? It's just we were watching a film, and it's getting late, and we've got school tomorrow . . . '

'That's fine,' said Noah. He was happy to leave. Ruby and her friends had made him feel like a circus freak. *Roll up, roll up. Come and see the amazing, stupid, tall man!*

'OK then, see you soon,' said Ruby. She mouthed 'sorry' at him again.

'Bye, then,' he said, turning towards the door. He didn't look back. As he headed down the stairs he thought he heard muffled giggling. He clenched his jaw and dug his nails into his palm to stop himself wanting to cry.

Once he was back home he went straight up to his room and lay down on his bed. He was furious, not just with Ruby, but with himself for ever believing that she could really like him. He grabbed hold of his pillow and hit it against the wall next to his bed, over and over, until he'd used up all his energy. It made him feel a little better. Then he sat down at his desk and sent a few emails to try to distract himself. It didn't work; he kept thinking about Ruby, asking himself what exactly he saw in her. He couldn't answer the question, but it didn't make him want her less. He took a look at her blog. Hundreds of people had checked out her new entry already and not one of them had questioned whether it was genuine. If anything, the opposite was true. Half the comments were from women desperate to get their hands on the crimson dress, many of them wanting geographical clues on where to find it. They seemed to think the whole thing was a game, a weird kind of treasure hunt.

– *I'm so so so so so so so so so sorry . . .*

The words materialised on his screen, with a ping, which made him jump. It was Ruby. He hadn't expected her to instant message him and the warm flutter in his gut told him he was pleased to hear from her, even though his brain knew he shouldn't have been. Still, he ignored her for a few minutes. He wanted her to know how hurt and angry he was.

– *Noah, are you there? Please don't be upset with me. I can explain.*

He waited another minute, then typed: *Hi, yes I'm here.*

– *Look, I know you must be upset and I know I'm the most horrible, meanest, cruellest, stupidest person in the whole world, but I really didn't mean to hurt you. Please believe me.*

– *So why did you?*

– *I don't know. It's hard to explain. I wasn't expecting you to come round before. I panicked. I do still like you.*

– *That's not good enough. You totally blanked me. You made me feel like a piece of crap.*

– *I know. I'm so sorry. Honestly. It's just that Mand and Hanni don't know about me and you and they'd have freaked if they found out like that.*

– *Why not? Are you ashamed of me?*

– *Course not. Don't be soft. You know what they're like. They don't know you like I do, do they? They can be a bit . . . you know.*

– *Are you going to tell them?*

– *Yes, of course, maybe not right now, but eventually. I promise. Have you told anyone?*

– *Only my sister.*

– *That's OK. But I think maybe you shouldn't tell anyone else for now.*

– *Why not?*

– Because we should maybe keep things to ourselves for a while. Take it slowly. If you're OK with that. I know you're good at keeping secrets.

– I'm not sure. Why?

– It's all too much right now, what with the blog exploding and everything. I just need a good friend, that's all. And you've been fantastic!

– Right. Just friends?

– Yes. With a few benefits. And only if you still want to be friends, that is. But it won't be forever, I promise.

– OK.

What else could he say? He was confused. Did she want to be his friend or did she want a secret relationship? He'd rather be with her secretly than not at all.

– You know, you're still the only person who knows about the blog and me. That makes you special.

– Really?

– Yeah. So what are you doing now? I mean before we messaged?

– Just going through some emails, nothing really. You?

– I was looking at my blog again. It's crazy. There's new comments going up every five minutes. Everyone wants my dress! People are saying they're going to find the charity shop tomorrow morning.

– I know. I saw it before.

– God, Noah, I still can't get my head round it all.

– Me neither.

– So do you forgive me then?

– Maybe.

– Only maybe?

– All right then, yes.

– Thanks, Noah. Can't wait to see you. I'll come round properly when I can.

– OK, can't wait to see you either.

– Night then.

– Sweet dreams.

Ruby went offline and Noah sat looking at the screen for a few moments, reading over their conversation, before logging out and switching off his computer. The conversation would be gone forever now, there would be no trace of it. But that was no different from any normal conversation, he supposed. He had a niggling feeling that he'd just been manipulated, although he didn't think Ruby had done it intentionally, or maliciously. She was all over the place, what with her exploding blog and her judgmental friends and her mixed-up feelings for him. The problem was, it meant he was all over the place too, and that wasn't somewhere he wanted to be. He liked his life to be ordered and structured. He liked knowing who his friends were, where he fitted, what he should be doing next. Sometimes, he thought, I feel like I'm alone on the moon, looking down at the world and everyone in it.

Chapter 18

The Daily Voice, April 15

Does Robyn live in your hood?

Do you know the girl behind Robyn Hood's blog? Are you one of her merry men? Or is she your Maid Marian? We want to unmask this outlaw, and we'll pay for information. Call our freephone number now.

Dee da da . . . Welcome back to the Sunshine Radio Breakfast Show. It's seven a.m. and today, once again, we're talking about Robyn Hood. That's the blogger, not the legendary guy with the bow and arrow, in case you've been asleep for the past few weeks. It seems the country has gone shoplifting mad. We've heard your opinions, several of them very strong indeed. Keep them coming. But now we want to hear what she has to say for herself. If you're listening, Robyn, please get in touch. We'd love to give you the chance to reveal what you think about your blog, shoplifting and the public response. Do you want to set the record straight? Give us a call!

Absolutely everybody appeared to want a piece of Robyn Hood. The newspapers were competing to be the first to find out who she was, and several radio stations broadcast pleas for her to phone in and chat live on air. Magazines offered her free makeovers and photo shoots if she'd only agree to an exclusive interview. There was even talk of turning her blog into a book. Of course, if people had known she was only fifteen, they might have been more cautious. But Ruby had never revealed her exact age in her blog, only that she was a 'young woman' and once, that she was wearing a school uniform.

The police were becoming impatient to find her too. While they couldn't prosecute someone for writing a blog, just because they didn't like what it said (not in this country, anyway), Robyn Hood was, perhaps unintentionally, encouraging copycat shoplifting. You could say she'd started a mini crime wave. In the past week alone, at least fourteen women and girls had been caught trying to steal expensive clothes from upmarket shops. Each time, they'd offered the same excuse: it wasn't really stealing because they were planning to donate the clothes to charity shops. They all claimed to be *the* Robyn Hood. It didn't take much investigation to prove that none of them was the mystery blogger; one clueless girl didn't even know how to switch on a computer. The Police Commissioner said the sooner Robyn was identified, the better it would be for everyone, and urged her to come forward, with the promise that she wouldn't be punished. They simply didn't have the manpower to deal with attention-seeking shoplifters. 'People must remember that theft remains a crime,' he added. 'And anyone caught doing it faces prosecution and a criminal record.'

The 'Robyn Hood Effect', as somebody in the media had christened it, was also having a great impact on charity shops. Sales were booming and there were queues around the block at those stores which blog readers had worked out might be selling the clothes Robyn had 'donated'. One morning, animal charity shops were besieged by women hunting for *that* red dress; of course they all left disappointed. The following day, while she was having breakfast (concerned that she was looking thin, her mother had begun insisting that she ate something every day before school), Ruby heard an interview on the radio with a woman from an organisation called the British Association of Charity Shops. The woman seemed flustered. She probably wasn't used to being grilled about criminal activity at seven o'clock in the morning. 'Our staff, who are mostly volunteers, many of them pensioners, are finding it hard to cope,' she said. That made Ruby feel guilty; she didn't want to cause problems for the charity shops. She thought of the sweet volunteers who'd taken her donations and wondered if they now suspected her.

'We greatly appreciate all public donations,' the woman continued, 'but clearly we do not want to be receiving and dealing in stolen goods. We're cooperating with the police. Our volunteers have been advised that if they suspect an item is stolen, they should not accept it. We won't be taking any brand-new items, unless you have proof of purchase, for the foreseeable future.'

People were even talking about Robyn Hood at school. From the details referred to in Ruby's blog, many kids had figured out that she must live locally, or even be one of their fellow pupils. Someone had come in one day with a T-shirt emblazoned with the slogan *I'm Robyn Hood* across the front, and had been sent home to change. The following day the head teacher had organised an emergency school assembly on the subject of shoplifting. After a lecture on the evils of stealing, he'd said that if Robyn Hood was indeed one of his pupils, she should make a confidential appointment to see him to talk about it. 'No one else needs to know who you are,' he said. 'We'd like to help you.' Nevertheless, any girl unfortunate enough to be sent to see the head teacher over the next few days became the subject of vicious gossip: 'I saw X waiting outside Mr Mason's office this morning . . . Do you think *she* could be Robyn Hood?'

'I think I'm going to hand myself in,' joked Amanda.

'Me too,' said Hanni. 'We should go together, say we're both Robyn Hood.'

Ruby shifted uncomfortably in her chair and pretended to be dozing. She could cope with situations like this by detaching herself from Robyn and telling herself they were talking about somebody else, which, in a way, they were. She was starting to grow used to the intense public interest in her blog. It no longer fazed her, or upset her. She found it exhilarating. Hungry for coverage, she now read the papers religiously online, and pored over her mum's copy at the kitchen table, (Pam was delighted to see that Ruby was finally taking an interest in current affairs), and listened to the radio whenever she was in her bedroom. She'd changed her radio alarm setting from a pure music station to one with phone-ins and discussions. If there was no mention of Robyn Hood, she felt a pang of disappointment.

But, at the same time, she was also beginning to feel paranoid, certain that at any moment she would be found out. She didn't believe that the police would be lenient with her, whatever they said. Whenever she wrote her blog – and it was becoming harder to think of things to say, now that she was relying almost entirely on her imagination – she felt anxious about posting it. If a car drove down her street while she was writing it, or she heard voices outside, it would make her jittery.

Since she had absolutely no idea how the internet

worked, she surmised that there must be invisible wires coming out of her computer, which passed through the roof of her house, were beamed into space, and eventually connected to a great big supercomputer, a hub, somewhere in the world. She assumed that the messages sent down these wires could be tracked, perhaps by satellite, or infra-red or some other sort of technology she'd seen used in a film. That meant that the authorities could identify her location within minutes and they could then send the secret services to swoop in through the windows and arrest her. Well, maybe not that last bit – that would be a bit over the top to catch a shoplifter – but they could alert the police and give them her name and address, anyway.

Noah told her it really didn't work like that – for one thing, the server wasn't based in her house – but she wouldn't be convinced. So he told her he could ensure nobody would ever catch up with her blog or track her down.

'How?' she asked. She knew she was unlikely to understand the explanation, but it seemed ungrateful not to appear interested.

'I can just keep changing your IP address and move from server to server,' he said. 'I'll make lots of mirror versions of your blog using different servers. Then, if I need to, I can shut down one IP address and move it to another one, which will already be active.'

'Right,' said Ruby. He might as well have told her

that he was going to put her blog on a rocket, fly it to Mars and translate it into Martian. 'That sounds good. And no one will ever be able to find out where I'm writing it from or who I am?'

'Not if you don't want them to,' he said. 'I promise.'

'OK,' she said, half-heartedly. 'How do you know all this techie stuff? Who taught you how to do it?'

'No one, I taught myself. And I swap tips with people, so I'm always learning. It's not as difficult as you might think.'

'Yeah, right. I don't think so – not with my brain,' she said. 'So that thing you're always working on, you know, your project, what exactly is it?'

Noah hesitated. 'Maybe I shouldn't say. It's not that I don't trust you, it's just really big, it could get me into tons of trouble.'

She looked at him quizzically. 'More trouble than I could get into?'

'Way, way more trouble. They could lock me up for it big time.'

'Seriously, Noah?' Ruby didn't want to show it, but she found the idea of Noah doing something risky, something illegal, rather thrilling. It made him seem intriguing, a little bit James Bond. She'd always thought he was super-straight and sensible.

'Yes, seriously. One hundred percent seriously.'

'So what are you doing? You don't have to tell me if you don't want to.'

He swallowed hard. 'OK, if you really want to know, I've found a way of hacking into websites. I've exposed all these security gaps, especially in the bank ones. If I wanted to, I could steal thousands of pounds.'

Oh my God, thought Ruby, we're not so different after all. 'Wow!' she said. 'That's scary.'

'Yeah. I'm trying to figure out the best way to reveal what I've found, without getting myself into deep trouble. Because if I'm doing it, you can bet someone else will be too.'

Ruby took his hand. She had the urge to kiss him, but things had been a little awkward in that department since she'd asked if they could cool their relationship. 'Don't worry, I swear I won't tell anyone.' It was a such a shame she couldn't, she thought, because that kind of information would definitely change her friends' opinions of Noah. It would make Amanda's eyes pop out of her head!

He smiled. 'Thanks. I can't believe I've told you. But it actually feels good to have said it out loud.'

'Hey, maybe you should write a blog about it!'

He laughed. 'I think I'll leave the words to you. I'll stick with the numbers.'

'So what are you going to do?'

'I don't know yet. I'm working on it. You?'

'God knows. Sorry to ask again but, Noah, you are sure that my blog is safe?'

'Yes, I swear.'

She should have felt reassured, but she didn't. The problem was, a big part of her *wanted* someone to find out who she really was. It had begun to dawn on her that she'd never enjoy any of the benefits of her blog's popularity unless people knew her real name. Robyn Hood was famous (or perhaps that should be infamous), but Ruby Collins was still a nobody, just a schoolgirl with an anxious mother, a rubbish dad, friends she couldn't entirely trust, and a super-complicated love life. She knew that soon people would grow tired of Robyn Hood and move on to the next thing. That's what always happened. So maybe this was her only chance to be someone? But if she did reveal herself, everybody would know that she was a thief. Her parents would be devastated and blame themselves, and her friends would hate her for not trusting them enough to confide in them. Plus, if she ended up with a criminal record she might not be able to go to university or get a good job.

It was, Ruby thought, a bit like admiring a scene inside a snow globe and knowing that, however much you want to, you can never be a part of it. You'll never be tiny enough to fit inside the glass, and even if you manage to shrink yourself down, trying to climb in would make it shatter into tiny pieces.

It made her feel restless and confused and, when she walked past the shops on her way home from school, she started to get that itchy sensation again, the one that made her want to go in and steal something.

Robyn Hood's Blog

I steal from expensive stores and give to charity shops

April 16

The newspapers are trying to find me. All I've got to say to them is: Blog Off.

Everyone seems to have a different idea about who I am. People are playing detective games, trying to piece together the 'clues' from my blog to find out my identity. But how do you know that any of what I've told you so far is the truth? Maybe I'm not a girl, but a boy, or a man. Maybe I'm 21 or 52 or 73. Maybe I steal things but don't give them to charity shops. Maybe I've never stolen anything at all in my life. Maybe I only said I wore a school uniform because I'm weird like that, or because I was going to a fancy-dress party. Maybe I'm actually a university student or a business woman. I could even be a teacher, or the Prime Minister. OK, probably not the Prime Minister but, hey, I might be already famous, too famous to write a blog using my real name. So famous that if I was caught shoplifting, my life would be over. Just think what people would say if it turned out I was an actor or a TV presenter?

What I don't get is, why do people care? Why does it

matter to you who I am or what I am? It never did before. And do you know what's funny? I bet if you really did know my identity, you wouldn't be interested in me at all.

Posted by Robyn Hood at 2.05 PM
Comments: 361
Followers: 5822
Blog Archive
Links

Chapter 19

'*It's seven-fifteen a.m. and you're listening to Sunshine Radio. We're delighted to say that we've got Robyn Hood on the line today. Yes, you heard right, THE Robyn Hood. She said she's a fan of the show and she's chosen to get in touch with US here at Sunshine Radio! Hello, Robyn, thanks so much for joining me.*'

'*Hi, Graham.*'

'*So how does it feel to finally go public?*'

'*It feels great! I'm so glad to talk to you. I've had enough of hiding. I want to get out there and show the world who I am.*'

'*Let's get back to basics. Tell me, Robyn, why did you decide to start writing your blog?*'

'*I did it because I wanted people to know how exciting it is to rip off the shops . . .*'

Ruby thought she must be in the middle of a nightmare. Robyn Hood was talking on the radio but she didn't sound like herself at all. Her voice was much higher in tone – a little squeaky to be frank – and she was saying things she would never have said. Things like, *'I'd love to have my own range in charity shops one day, that's a cool idea, Graham'* and *'Sure, I might think about posing for one of the men's magazines with only a bow and arrow, as long as it was tasteful'*. But this couldn't be a nightmare because her eyes were open, and her arm felt numb because she'd been lying on it, and she could see light streaming in through the gap in the curtains. It couldn't be a nightmare because she was fully conscious, aware that she was lying in bed, and she could tell that her mouth wasn't moving, even though the voice kept talking. *'I'm nineteen, really,'* it was saying. *'Saying I was a schoolgirl was a red herring. I was teasing people, you know . . .'*

'Oh God!' Ruby wrenched her duvet away from her body and threw it from her bed on to the floor. 'Shut up! Shut up!' She wanted to make the voice stop but she also felt compelled to listen to it. This was worse than any nightmare. Somebody was hijacking her blog live on the radio, pretending to be her, and worse, changing everyone's opinions about her. If the radio station believed the girl they were interviewing was Robyn Hood – and hadn't they done any proper checks? – then so would the listeners. She knew it was partly her own fault for putting misleading information in her blog, information that meant anybody could now justifiably claim to be Robyn Hood. But she'd only done that to make a point, to protect herself. Instead, she was losing control of her own identity, of her 'brand' – for that was what Robyn Hood had become. There were even new blogs springing up all over the web, purporting to be written by Robyn Hood. Soon, nobody would remember which was the original one. And who would care?

Ruby was running late for school, but that didn't matter. She couldn't leave things as they were. Hurriedly, she logged into her blog and, in huge capital letters typed.

I AM THE REAL ROBYN HOOD. THE ONLY ONE. I WAS NOT ON SUNSHINE RADIO THIS MORNING. I HAVE NEVER BEEN ON ANY RADIO STATION OR ANY TV SHOW. WHOEVER THAT GIRL WAS, SHE WAS A FAKE.

THIS IS MY ONLY BLOG. IGNORE THE OTHERS. PLEASE DON'T BELIEVE ANYTHING YOU READ IN THE PAPERS OR HEAR ON THE RADIO ABOUT ME. I AM A GIRL. I AM FIFTEEN YEARS OLD. I STILL GO TO SCHOOL. I PROMISE I WILL TELL YOU MORE ABOUT ME WHEN I'M READY. SOON.

After typing and posting her message, she felt so wound up, she wasn't sure what to do with herself. She paced around her bedroom a few times, then climbed into the shower and stood under the stream of hot water until her skin was red and blotchy. She looked at her watch: it was almost eight o'clock. She wasn't dressed, she hadn't had breakfast, and Hanni would be waiting for her. Maybe she wouldn't go to school after all. It was pointless; there was no way she'd be able to concentrate.

She texted Hanni: *Gt period pn. Cvr 4 me. CU ltr.* Then she put on her school uniform anyway, because there was no way her mum would let her off school, not unless she had a temperature of a hundred and five, or was covered in boils, or was coughing up her lungs (or probably, all three at once). She'd make out that she was going to school as usual, hang out somewhere for a while, and then, when she was sure Mum had gone to work, she'd go back home. She looked out of the window. Noah had just left his house and was walking down his garden path, with his horrible brown nylon rucksack strapped to his back. He turned and looked up at her, and waved.

'Wait!' she mouthed.

He stopped, suddenly, and his rucksack bounced awkwardly, jarring against him. Even from the vantage point of her bedroom window, Ruby could tell he looked surprised and confused. Although he didn't like it, he'd accepted that he and Ruby wouldn't walk to school together because she always had to go with

Hanni. Now, he'd be wondering whether she'd changed her mind, and why.

'I'm coming down,' she motioned. 'Wait for me, please!' She grabbed her school bag and rushed down the stairs, two at a time. 'Mum,' she shouted, as she opened the front door, 'I'm running late, I haven't got time for breakfast this morning. Gotta go, sorry! Bye!' Before her mother had a chance to reply, she had slammed the door shut behind her.

'Hey, what's up?' said Noah, as she approached him. He kissed her on the cheek and they hugged. 'Is everything OK?'

'Not really, I'm in a bit of a state,' she said. She wondered if he'd noticed that she hadn't even straightened her hair, like she usually did. She must have looked terrible. 'Thanks for waiting for me. Have you got a couple of minutes?' He nodded. 'Can we just go round the corner, so Mum can't see us? I'm not going to school this morning.'

They sat on a wall outside someone's house and she told him about the fake Robyn Hood on the radio, and the fake bloggers, and her fears that she was now losing control of her own blog. She didn't tell him she was also afraid she was losing control of herself, that she was feeling the urge to shoplift again. 'It's really getting me down and I don't know what to do about it,' she said. 'I don't want other people getting famous because of my blog. I want people to know about me, who I am. I'm the one who wrote it. It's all my thoughts and feelings.'

'Yeah, but if you come forward then everyone will know about your stealing. You might get a criminal record. What about your parents? What about school? What about your mates?'

'I know all that. But maybe I don't care any more. Maybe it's worth it. This could be my only chance in the whole of my life to make it big, to have people take notice of me. Everyone soon forgets why you're famous, anyway. In the end they just remember your name, not why they know it.'

'I don't think it's a good idea, Rubes,' he said. He held out his hand to her. She glanced around, self-consciously, and took it, loosely.

'But if I don't come out, someone else is going to get all my publicity!' she cried, then laughed out loud at herself. 'God, I sound like a real diva now, I know. Sorry. It's just the girl on the radio, she was such a bimbo. I don't want people thinking I'm like her.'

'But you didn't start the blog to get famous, did you?'

'Course not. I write a blog because it means I can be me, without being me. It means I can confess everything, blurt it all out, without getting into trouble. I didn't dream anybody would read it, let alone that all this would happen. But now it has happened, maybe it's fate. I can't make it go back to the way it was.'

'Honestly, you don't have to do anything,' he

pleaded. 'It'll all die down soon. I can help you make Robyn Hood disappear, and start up a new blog for you, if that's what you'd like. You don't have to get into trouble with anyone. I'll help you make it so you can just be you again.'

'But I don't want to be plain old Ruby Collins again,' she said, dropping his hand. 'I wish you understood that.'

Chapter 20

Pam was at her office desk, sorting through her emails, when her phone rang.

'Hello, is this Mrs Collins, Mrs Pam Collins?' said a voice she didn't recognise. An officious, rather nasal voice, Pam thought. 'Yes, speaking,' she said brightly.

'Mrs Collins, my name is Bob Owen. I'm the head of security at Kelly's Department Store. I'm afraid we've got your daughter here. She's been caught shoplifting.'

Pam didn't understand. 'No, I'm sorry, there must be some mistake. My daughter is at school today. You must have the wrong number. Or the wrong name.'

'Is your daughter's name Ruby, Mrs Collins? Is she fifteen years old?'

'Yes . . . but it's not possible. I saw her leave for school myself. She was wearing her uniform.'

'Mrs Collins, I regret to tell you it's definitely not a mistake. Ruby is indeed wearing a school uniform. She gave us this number herself. She's been very cooperative. If you like, we can put her on the phone for you to confirm it.'

'Yes, please,' said Pam. She still believed that this might be a hideous error, and that some other girl would come on the line, so she could say, 'But you're not my daughter!'

There was a click and then Pam heard, 'Muuuuum,' in between heavy sobs and what sounded like, 'I'm so sorry. So sorry.' It was definitely Ruby's voice, however much Pam wanted it not to be. Now she felt nauseous.

'It's OK,' she said, although she didn't mean it.

Bob Owen came back on the line. 'Was that your daughter Ruby?'

'Yes,' said Pam. 'I still don't understand. I'm sure there's an explanation.'

'I think you should come down to the store now, Mrs Collins, if that's possible. We've already tried to contact Mr Collins, but he's unobtainable.'

No change there, then, Pam thought. It was selfish, but it hurt that Ruby had suggested calling him first. What did he ever do for her, except let her down? 'Yes,' she said. 'I'm at work. I'll just let my manager know and then I'll be straight there.'

Pam had only ever been into Kelly's at sale time, and only then to buy gifts. She found the store far too expensive and frivolous for her needs and she couldn't imagine what Ruby was doing there, when she should have been at school. Bob Owen had told her he'd meet her at the office at the back, by the changing rooms, and as she walked past rows and rows of beautifully folded cashmere scarves, jewellery and cosmetics, she thought about Ruby, and wondered whether she had been a bad mother. Ruby had always been a good girl, not perfect, but she'd never been a worry, never got into drugs or joyriding or any of the other things teenagers might do.

Had something changed, something that she hadn't noticed? Yes, Ruby had been quiet lately, caught up in her thoughts, and she'd suddenly become interested in the news, which hadn't preoccupied her before, but Pam had thought that was a good development, that it meant she was growing up and becoming aware of the world around her. She must have heard about all that Robyn Hood stuff. Pam had read about copycat shopliftings and thought how foolish those girls were; could Ruby have been influenced by them? Was it peer pressure that had turned her into a thief? The media had a lot to answer for, she thought.

Bob Owen was waiting for her by the information desk, just as he'd said he would be. He was a tall man, wearing a dark suit, not a uniform, as she'd expected, and he had a rather world-weary expression on his face.

'Mrs Collins?' he said.

'Yes,' said Pam. She tried to smile, and took his hand

when it was offered to her, although she didn't feel much like shaking it.

'Follow me, please,' he said.

Without another word he led her into a back office. Ruby was sitting on a chair, behind a desk, her head in her hands. She looked up when Pam came in. Her eyes were puffy and red, and it was obvious she'd been crying for a long time.

'Mum,' she said.

Pam wanted to be angry, to shake her and say, 'What on earth have you been doing?' She tried to look stern, but she couldn't. Ruby was still her baby, her only child, and all she could do was walk over to her daughter and hug her, while she sobbed quietly in her arms.

'Mrs Collins,' said Mr Owen, pulling up another chair. 'We need to discuss what happened.'

Pam let Ruby go. 'Of course,' she said.

'Ruby stole some hair accessories and a lipstick,' he said. 'We found them in her bag when she tried to exit the store. We've got it all on CCTV, if you'd like to see.'

He pointed to a monitor on the desk and Pam watched the grainy footage of a girl who was unmistakably Ruby, walking around the shop floor, picking things up and then putting them down. At one point, she appeared to look right into the camera, and then she looked away, and put something into her school bag. This went on for a few minutes, until Ruby walked out of view.

'This is when we apprehended her,' said Mr Owen.

He pointed to the screen, and Ruby came back into the frame. She was being led by a security guard, her hands above her head, as she was marched through the store in front of the other customers. When Ruby witnessed this, her humiliation on film, her sobs grew louder.

Mr Owen opened a drawer and took out a plastic bag containing the items he'd talked about: some sparkly, jewelled hair slides, and a lipstick in a gold tube. 'They're worth about thirty pounds,' he said. 'She's removed the price tags, which constitutes criminal damage, so they need to be paid for.' Pam nodded. 'You're lucky it's not more, or we'd have called in the police. And as she hasn't been violent, either, or foul-mouthed, or tried to run, we've decided we're going to let her off with a warning.'

'Thank goodness,' said Pam. 'Thank you so much. I am absolutely sure it's the first and last time she'll ever do this.'

'Good,' said Mr Owen. 'She'll also be banned from the store for the period of a year. If she tries to enter, we can prosecute her for trespass.'

Ruby half climbed up from her chair, then sat back down again. 'But I told you, I want you to call the police,' said Ruby, her voice cracking. 'It's not the first time. I've done it loads of times. I've done it here!'

'Sorry?' said Pam.

'Not this again,' said Mr Owen, impatiently. 'She keeps saying she wants me to involve the police because she wants to confess to being that Robyn Hood girl, the one in the news. I can't tell you how many times I've heard that over the past few weeks. It's extremely tiresome.'

'But I am Robyn Hood,' said Ruby. 'I can prove it.'

'Don't be ridiculous,' said Pam. She wanted to pay for the goods (the money could come out of Ruby's pocket money), and then get Ruby out of there, and home, as quickly as possible.

Ruby started to cry again, but she had no tears left. What came out was more of a snotty snivel. 'Why won't anyone believe me?'

'I am not prepared to waste police time,' Mr Owen said. 'And believe you me, you wouldn't get such soft treatment from them.' He studied Ruby closely. 'You look like a nice girl, clearly you're from a nice family. I'm guessing you're going to do fairly well in your GCSEs, maybe go to university. Well, however many A stars you think you are going to get, with a conviction for shoplifting you would have a criminal record too. And that would make it very hard for you ever to get a job.'

Ruby sighed loudly. 'I don't care. I don't need a job. I am Robyn Hood. I am the mystery blogger. Listen . . . ' She started to try to recite portions of the blog, but she was in such a state she got her words muddled up.

'Anybody could go on the web and learn a blog off by heart,' said Mr Owen. 'Mrs Collins, I suggest you take your daughter home and perhaps find someone for her to talk to.'

Pam nodded. Poor Ruby, she was such a mess. How could she, as her mother, not have realised? She got up and put her hand on Ruby's shoulder. 'Come on,' she said. 'We need to go home now. And we need to talk to your father.' She paid for Ruby's stolen items and then, in silence, led her daughter back through the store to the exit. Ruby walked with her head down, sulking, just like she did when she was three and had been told off.

Pam's car was parked in the car park. She tried to give her daughter a hug across the seat, but Ruby sat stiffly and wouldn't respond.

'Why don't you believe me?' she said. 'Don't you understand? I wanted to get caught. I took that stuff deliberately in front of the cameras, so they'd catch me and get the police, and I could reveal who I was. If I'd really wanted to take that stuff and get away with it, it would have been easy. I've done it loads of times before. Just read my blog, you'll see.'

'Don't talk nonsense, Ruby,' said Pam.

'Is it so hard to believe that I could possibly write that blog? Aren't I smart enough? Aren't I interesting enough?'

'You're really scaring me,' said Pam. 'I'm going to ring your dad.'

Chapter 21

Two hours later, Ruby's family was gathered in her kitchen, the atmosphere so heavy with tension and emotion that it formed an almost visible cloud. Pam and James could barely look at one another and Ruby was monosyllabic. She was exhausted and angry that, despite her repeated protests, nobody would believe her claim. She'd hoped her dad would be more understanding but, if anything, he was even less sympathetic than her mum. It didn't help that he was irritated he'd been pulled out of an important business meeting. He kept telling Ruby how stupid she was, and how disappointed he was in her behaviour. He said he and her mum would have to discuss the appropriate punishment, but it was likely that at the very least, she'd be grounded. They hadn't decided whether or not to inform the school; her truancy still needed to be explained.

'What I don't understand is why you need to shoplift,' he said, sighing deeply. 'I've always given you everything you could ever want, haven't I? I buy you nice things all the time.'

Ruby nodded. 'I know, Dad. It's not about that. Read the blog, then you'll see.'

'As for this Robyn Hood nonsense, you should be a big girl and take responsibility for what you've done, instead of finding excuses and making up stories.'

'It's not an excuse Dad,' Ruby said, close to tears again. 'It's the truth. Please, let me prove it.'

'OK, so let's see some of these things you've stolen, then.'

'I don't keep any of them. I give them all to charity shops, that's the whole point. Don't you read the papers? Come down to the cancer charity shop with me now, or any of them. The volunteers all know me! I've always been careful to go to lots of different shops, so no one suspects, but if I tell them who I am and what I brought in, they'll remember. I know they will!'

'Of course they will,' said Pam. 'We're always taking things in there.'

'Wait!' cried Ruby, desperately trying to think. 'Actually, I do have some earrings, that I took when we were shopping for Helen. Dad, remember, that jewellery shop, the expensive one? I took these amazing pendant earrings and the charity shop wouldn't have them because they were for pierced ears.'

He laughed. 'You're expecting me to believe that you stole pricey jewellery from right under my nose? Come on then, let's see these earrings.'

'OK. And then you can ring the shop and ask if they remember them going missing. They're bound to remember. I've got them upstairs . . . They're . . .' She whirled around in frustration. Of course, she didn't have the earrings any more – she'd given them to Noah to hide. 'Look, I know this sounds like an excuse, but I don't have them now. I can get them for you later, I promise. In the meantime, please just bring me your laptop and I'll show you my blog. When you read it, you'll know I'm telling the truth.'

Exasperated, James went to fetch his briefcase from the hall. 'OK,' he said, when he returned. 'Here's my laptop. Now, get this silly nonsense over with once and for all.' He placed it on the table, brought up the internet and slid it across the table to Ruby.

Ruby smiled. She felt re-energised, the adrenalin surging back to her body. I'll show them, she thought. Now they'll see! She found the blog log-in page and typed in her password, pushing return with a triumphant prod of her thumb.

Username or Password not recognised.

She must have been too hasty and mis-typed. She tried again.

Username or Password not recognised.

It wasn't possible. She knew her username and password as well as her own name and date or birth. 'I think there must be a fault,' she pleaded. 'Something wrong with the internet!' She saw her parents roll their eyes at each other. 'Please let me bring up my blog from the outside, so at least I can show you it and talk you through it.'

Shaking, she typed in her blog's URL address and pressed return.

This page does not exist.

This couldn't be happening. Where was her blog? She was in a blind panic now. Had the police taken it down, or the internet company, or the Government, maybe? What if she did a Google search? There it was, first in the results . . . but why wouldn't it load? All the other fake Robyn Hood sites were still there, all the articles linking to her blog, but where was her blog?

And then she understood. It was Noah. It must have been Noah. Only he could have taken down the blog. Only he had a reason to.

'I've got to go!' she announced, jumping up from the table and rushing into the hall. 'Back in a minute . . . '

'Where do you think you're going, young lady?' she heard her Mum shout, as she opened the front door. 'Stop!'

She was out in the street before she thought to look at her watch. Three o'clock. It was a school day, would

Noah even be home yet? Maybe, if he had a free last period. She looked up at his window, but there was no sign of him. Her parents would be coming after her, any moment. She had to think. She ran down to the corner of the street, so she was out of sight. How long did she have before they came out looking for her? Thank God her mobile was in her pocket.

Whr r u? she texted. *I nd 2 spk 2 u now!*

Two long minutes passed. Then: *On my way hm frm schl. 1 min. u ok?*

She knew exactly which way he would be walking, so she started towards him, hoping to head him off before he turned into their cul-de-sac. It can't have been more than a few seconds before she saw him coming towards her. He was walking fast, frantically swinging his arms to keep up speed.

She ran up to him, so angry that she wanted to hit him. 'How could you? How could you?'

Even though she didn't say, he knew what she meant. He'd been waiting for this. 'I'm so sorry, but I took it down to protect you. I thought you were going to do something stupid.'

'You're too late,' she said, tearfully. 'I already did. And you've made it worse.'

She told him about Kelly's. 'Now my parents think I'm a freak, as well as a thief and a liar.'

'Oh Rubes,' he said. He tried to put his arm around her, but she backed away. 'I'm sorry. I was trying to help because I care, honest I was.'

'But it's my blog, my words, my life! You had no right to take it down like that.'

'I know, I'm sorry. I'll put it back up for you, I promise.'

'Good,' she said. 'Because as soon as you do, I'm going to confess everything. First I can tell my parents – and you can back me up. And then in the blog. After that, people will have to believe me.'

Noah sighed. 'You're making a mistake . . .'

'And another thing,' said Ruby. 'You know those earrings I asked you to take for me? I really appreciated you doing that, but I need them back now. To show my dad.'

Noah hesitated. 'The thing is, I don't have them,' he said. 'Sorry, Rubes, but I got rid of them. I didn't want anyone else to find them.'

'You've got to be kidding! Where are they?'

'I threw them out. They'll be on a landfill site somewhere now. Gone forever. Sorry.'

'Noooooo! They're my only proof.'

'You don't need proof, Ruby. Listen, I've been thinking about this and I've got an idea. You could come forward about the blog, reveal yourself, but say it was all made up, like a story. That way you'll get all the credit for writing the blog without getting into trouble with anyone. I've got all the computer evidence, the whole history, so they'll know it was really you who started the blog.'

'So I'll be a stupid liar, a fantasist, instead of a thief? My parents already think I'm losing it. And I've been caught shoplifting twice now. The people at Zenda and Kelly's will recognise me and they'll say they know I really did it.'

'I doubt it, they must catch hundreds of shoplifters every week. And if they do, you can say it was just for research or to get noticed. We can think of something. I'll help you. We can work it out together.'

'I don't know,' she said. 'I need time to think about it.'

'OK,' said Noah. 'But do you forgive me now?'

'Maybe,' she said, giving him a little smile.

He moved to hug her again, and this time she let him. She buried her face in his chest and breathed him in, the smell and the feel of him. She sensed how small her body was against his, his long arms firmly wrapped around her waist, and it made her feel safe, protected, as if everything was going to work out. Then she gazed up at him and he gave her *that* slightly squinty look from beneath *those* eyelashes, the look that turned her insides to jelly. The hug turned into a kiss, a long, slow comforting kiss that she didn't want to end.

'I'd better go home and face the music,' she said eventually, pulling herself away. She could still feel the sensation of his lips on hers. It would be so easy to fall back into that kiss. 'I promise I'll call you later.'

'Do,' said Noah. 'Remember, I'll help you any way I can. We can work it out together.'

She nodded. 'Thanks.'

Later that night, after her parents had screamed and shouted until they had no voices left, her dad had gone home and her mum had sent her to her room like a kid, Ruby lay fully clothed on her bed and thought about what to do. Noah's idea was attractive, because it meant she could still take the credit for her blog without owning up to being a compulsive thief, but something about it didn't feel right. The blog was hers, the vehicle for her personal thoughts and feelings (at least, until the point she'd felt she had to lie to keep her readers happy). If she claimed it had all been a fantasy, then she'd be denying who she really was. She'd spent too long doing that already, trying to fit in with her friends, trying to be the person her parents wanted her to be. Just for once, she had to be true to herself.

She didn't feel like talking, and this seemed a little too important for a quick text, so she opened up a new email. *Sorry Noah*, she wrote. *Thank you for trying to help. But I'm going to do it my way. xx*

Chapter 22

The following morning, Ruby awoke at seven to the thumping bass of a song she pretended to like but secretly hated. Her eyes still welded shut, she leaned across the bed and pressed the snooze button, sending herself into a fitful doze. When she woke up again, at seven-fifteen, it was to the drone of the weather report. She punched the radio off, feeling drowsy and bad-tempered. She'd hardly had any rest. It had taken her several hours to drop off and then she'd slept badly, her dreams fragmented and dark. She had woken several times in the night with a sensation of dread that made her heart pound wildly. Once, she felt so alone and so afraid that she had thought of texting Noah for comfort, but it had been five a.m., and he'd only have tried to talk her out of her plans.

She kicked off her duvet and swung her feet on to the

matted fibres of the rug below. From downstairs she could hear the whirr of the toaster and the whine of muffled voices on breakfast television. Mum was going to work early for a meeting; she'd told Ruby the night before, even though they weren't really speaking. She'd stood in the hall just outside Ruby's bedroom and shouted this information to her through the locked door. Ruby hadn't responded because she was too upset and angry to speak and her voice had been caught in her throat.

Her mother was shouting to her again now. 'I'm going to work, love. I've left your dinner money on the side,' and this time Ruby intended to reply, but before she could, she heard the front door slam shut. When she was younger, Mum always used to make Ruby come down and kiss her goodbye, but she'd long since given up trying. Ruby couldn't remember when she'd last kissed her mother. On Mother's Day, probably. It was what you did, like buying flowers and a card that said, *You're the best mum in the world*, and managing to keep a straight face when she opened it. The funny thing was, she could have done with a hug from Mum now.

Before she got ready for school she checked her emails. There was nothing from Noah. Why hadn't he replied? He kept his computer on twenty-four seven, and he received his messages on his phone too, so she was absolutely certain he had read her email, very likely only a few minutes after she'd sent it. Her blog wasn't back up either. She didn't know what to think. Was there something wrong with his internet connection? Was he was annoyed with her for not wanting to follow his advice? But if so, then why hadn't he just told her? Maybe he'd just had to rush out early and hadn't had time. She'd corner him at school and talk to him about it, she decided. That way she could explain properly, discuss her reasons with him, even persuade him to help her. Revealing herself wouldn't be easy; there were simply so many unknowns. It would be good to have someone she could confide in and talk things through with, an ally.

After she had washed her face and pulled her hair into a ponytail, she decided to squeeze the two large zits that had formed overnight on either side of her chin. It was a mistake. Neither of them had yet come to a head, so there was no satisfying whooshing sound as the pressure released, and when she had finished, there was more blood than pus in the tissue. Now she felt ugly and self-conscious too. Her mother had left a cup of coffee out for her in the kitchen. It was lukewarm and bitter, despite the sugars, so she abandoned it on the counter.

Noah wasn't at school when she arrived, which was weird because he was never later than her. It was possible that he was ill, she thought, but he hadn't said anything about not feeling well yesterday. Perhaps it was one of those bugs that comes on suddenly in the night. She felt the glands at the sides of the neck, hoping she hadn't caught it. She did feel a little off-colour, but that could just have been nerves, or lack of sleep. It was also possible that Noah had an appointment she wasn't aware of, at the dentist or optician, something that couldn't be fitted in after school and was too boring to have mentioned. She texted him a couple of times during the morning, between lessons, to ask where he was, but he didn't reply. His phone was probably switched off, or out of reach. She grasped for a simple explanation, pushing aside her fears that something had happened to Noah, or that he was avoiding her. She wasn't sure which would be worse. The longer she went without hearing from him, the more worried and frustrated she became. She was desperate to talk to him. If she was going to do it, do *it*, she didn't want to do it without him.

Lunch break came and still there was no sign of Noah. She texted him: *R U OK? x*. Again, he didn't reply. He must really be angry with me, she decided, and she felt a pang of something that was a little like fear.

'What's up?' asked Hanni, for the sixth or seventh time. 'You seem really quiet today. Moody.'

'Nothing, I'm fine, just tired,' said Ruby, rubbing her eyes to make the point. She wanted to tell Hanni what was going on – her friends deserved to know the truth before she went public with it – but she had no idea how to broach the subject, or how they might react. 'Just stuff with my mum and dad. I'll tell you later,' she added, guiltily, and Hanni gave her a rather smug, conspiratorial smile, which said, 'I knew there was more to it.'

Ross walked past them and nodded, as if he couldn't quite bring himself to blank Ruby but wouldn't deign to speak to her now either. She nodded back, surprised at how little his indifference hurt. Nothing had ever been said; it hadn't been a relationship with a proper beginning or a middle, so perhaps it was fitting that there hadn't been a definite end either. It had just drifted in and out of existence.

'Are you all right? About him, I mean,' said Hanni, gesturing towards Ross. She put her hand on Ruby's shoulder.

'Course, why wouldn't I be?'

'Only because you had a thing with him. And I heard he was seeing someone else now.'

'Is he? Good for him. I really don't mind, I'm not just saying it.' I've got someone else too, she thought. If only she could find a way to tell Hanni.

'Sure, hon,' said Hanni, unconvinced. 'Hey, there's Mand.' She beckoned their friend over. 'Where have you been?'

'Just talking to a couple of sixth-form lads. Hey, guess what they told me: did you know they've got that Robyn Hood girl?'

'What, again?' said Hanni. 'Who is it this time? Don't tell me: your friend's friend's second cousin's sister? Or maybe it's Miss Duncan.'

Amanda groaned. 'No, seriously, someone tweeted it earlier. It's all over the web. The real deal, they said. It was even on the news and everything. So it must be true.'

Ruby felt sick. Yet another girl had made a false confession, and this time it sounded like she was being taken seriously. How long would it be before this girl was found to be a fraud too? A few hours? A few days? People were going to get fed up and lose interest soon, she was certain of it. There was already less talk, fewer stories. Maybe she'd missed her moment. Why hadn't she insisted on the police coming to Kelly's yesterday? She should have made a bigger fuss, broken something, hit that security guard, if that was what it took. Even if she hadn't gone that far, why hadn't she demanded that her parents take her straight to the police station, instead of letting them rant at her until she went to bed? It really wasn't just about being famous any more, it was about revealing the truth, about making things right. 'So who is it then?' she asked.

'I dunno,' said Amanda. 'Sorry. All I know is someone handed themselves in to the police this morning and said they were Robyn Hood.'

'Stupid,' said Hanni. 'Why go to the police and not the papers? Or the TV? That's what I'd do. Didn't they already say she wouldn't get done for anything?'

Amanda shrugged. 'It'll probably turn out to be some nutter, like those people who confess to murders they didn't do. But hey, maybe this time it really is Robyn Hood, like they're saying. Her blog's disappeared. I had a look before. No sign of it. Weird, huh?'

'Oh right,' said Ruby, somehow managing to control her voice. 'That is strange. Listen, I need the loo. I'll see you both in French, OK?'

'Sure, hon, said Amanda. 'I'll save you a seat.'

You weren't supposed to go into the classrooms during break-time, but Ruby didn't care. All she could think about was getting to a PC so she could find out more about the new Robyn Hood pretender. There were some in the lab, near her classroom – that wasn't usually locked. With luck, she'd be able to let herself in, unnoticed. She waited until the corridor was clear and then tried the door. It opened. Without turning on the light, she made her way over to the computer furthest from the door and woke it up. Then she brought up the internet and typed *Robyn Hood* into a search engine. There were, it said, 183,471 results, but it was only the most recent ones that interested Ruby.

Robyn Hood unmasked, read the headline on a supposedly reliable gossip news site.

Unconfirmed reports suggest that the mystery blogger, Robyn Hood, is in police custody. A police source revealed that a teenager came forward this morning and is now helping them with their inquiries . . .

Before she could read on, the door opened behind her, making her jump, and the fluorescent strip light flickered into life above her head. Blinking hard against the glare, she closed down the screen as quickly as she could.

'Who's in here?' said a woman in a sharp tone.

Ruby turned around on her chair, her pulse rising. Her eyes were still adjusting to the light, but from the woman's tall, rather bulky silhouette she could tell that it was Mrs Robins, who taught ICT. That was a stroke of luck. She was OK for a teacher, if anything a bit too soft. 'Me, Mrs Robins,' she said, getting up from her chair. 'It's Ruby Collins from year eleven.'

'What are you doing in here at lunchtime, Ruby?'

'I was doing some research,' said Ruby, telling the truth.

'I see. Well, you shouldn't really be in here without permission.'

'I know. Sorry, Mrs Robins.'

'And it's not good for your eyes to use the computer in the dark. Have you finished now?'

'Er, yeah. Well, um, I was also going to send an email, to a friend who isn't in school. I was worried about him and he's not replying to my texts.'

'Who, Ruby?'

'Noah Baker, Mrs Robins.'

'I didn't know you were friends with Noah, dear,' she said, looking Ruby up and down. 'I'm afraid his mother called in earlier. There's been a death in the family. He probably won't be in for a few days, she said.'

'Oh,' exclaimed Ruby, shocked by an explanation she

hadn't even considered. It made her feel sick and panicky. Thoughts galloped through her mind, so fast that she couldn't keep up. Noah hadn't mentioned that anyone was ill. It must have been sudden, then. Was it someone close? She wasn't even sure if he still had any grandparents. Someone young? One of his sisters? Had there been an accident? At least *he* was OK. 'I didn't realise,' she said. 'Who's died?'

'His mother didn't say,' said Mrs Robins. 'Don't worry, dear, I'm sure he'll be in touch with you later.' She looked at her watch. 'Now, lessons are about to start again. You'd better get back to your classroom.'

The afternoon seemed interminable. They always did to Ruby, but this one surely was the longest ever. She was so anxious that she couldn't concentrate on anything. She had a long list of things she wanted to do, important things, and hearing Mr Lister bang on about the causes of the Second World War was not on it. She was by turns worried about Noah and concerned for herself. Why hadn't he told her someone had died? Didn't he trust her enough? Or was it just a story, a cover, because he was avoiding her? And what should she do about her plans? Put them on hold until she heard from him? But what if he was away for days? What if he didn't contact her at all? What if he was in a bad way? It wouldn't be fair. No, she decided, she'd made her mind up and she couldn't change it. She had to do it today, with or without him.

She thought about sneaking out before the final period of the day, but it wasn't worth the risk of ending up in detention and having to stay in school even later. So she waited until the final bell, grabbed her things from her locker and ran out of the back doors, before Hanni or Amanda or any of her other friends could catch up with her. She was lucky. The bus came straight away and within minutes had deposited her on the high street, exactly where she wanted to be. This was what she'd been planning: her final shoplifting spree. One last, delicious steal. She had always known that once her identity was revealed she wouldn't be able to do it again; that was the price she'd pay. But, when people knew *she* was the blogger, and not that stupid imposter who was wasting everyone's time, she wouldn't need to do it again, she was sure of that. She wanted things to be neat, symmetrical, so she chose to return to the scene of her very first crime, the store from which she had stolen the tights. This time she would take something good, something substantial. If she was caught in the act she would make sure the police were called to arrest her. She would do whatever it took: swear, be disrespectful, try to run. Yet, she wouldn't get caught deliberately. She had to do it properly, using everything she'd learned and according to the rules she'd devised. Only one detail would be different: there would be no charity shop donation. If fate decreed that she got away with her crime, as she had so many times before, she would go home, show her mum what she'd stolen and then force her to take her to the police station.

She was surprised not to feel the usual thrill of anticipation as she walked into the store, only a dull, empty sensation in the pit of her stomach. Her heartbeat barely increased at all and her palms remained dry and cold. It was like waking up on Christmas morning and realising, with disappointment, that you're not excited because you're no longer a kid, and you don't believe in Santa Claus. Maybe it was because she'd been thinking about it too much, but it felt like she was doing a job that needed to be done, merely going through the motions. She scoped the shop, noting the position of the shop assistants and the cameras, and decided on her target: a long, grey wool cardigan with silver buttons. It was something she might like to wear, although she knew she never would. The cardigan was on a hanger, along with several others, in various sizes. She paused to rifle through them, choosing one in her size – not that it mattered – and laying it over her arm so that the hanger swung perilously from its shoulders. She took it into the unmanned changing room, along with a few other items that she casually picked up en route. This shop really is far too easy to steal from, she thought. Staff who can't be bothered, no security guard, no changing-room assistants. I bet there isn't even any film in those cameras. Shame I won't be coming back.

She had brought a pair of pliers with her, from the toolkit in the garage, so she could remove the security tag. But, as she set to work, it struck her that she'd be better off leaving the tag on. She needed proof that she was a thief, and without its security tag the cardigan wouldn't do as a piece of evidence. So she put the pliers away and, with its tag still attached, stuffed the cardigan into her bag and left the changing room. Then she loitered in the shop until she saw some other shoppers head for the exit. The idea was to blend into the group, so that when the alarm went off at the door, it wouldn't be obvious who had triggered it. In the confusion, she'd be able to get away unnoticed. She managed to wedge herself between two women, one a doddery old lady, and one middle-aged. Her daughter, probably. They both wore hats and matching gloves and moved painfully slowly. 'Sorry in advance,' muttered Ruby, unintelligibly to her innocent escorts, as they all reached the security barrier at the exit. She took a deep breath and held it in, waiting for the wail of the siren, practically willing it, but it didn't come. The automatic doors slid open and closed behind her, in graceful silence. As she stepped outside, all she could hear was the chatter of shoppers on the street and the low moan of passing traffic. She laughed to herself, unsure whether to be relieved or disappointed. The tag must have been faulty, or the barriers broken. It was surely a sign, but of what she couldn't say.

Ruby walked home briskly, so briskly that she didn't take in the local paper sandwich board outside the newsagent, which displayed the headline: *Robyn Hood Held. More details inside.* All she could think about was reaching home and preparing herself before Mum came back from work. As she put the key into the lock she twisted her head around to look up at Noah's bedroom. He wasn't at the window and the lights were off in his room. The whole house looked dark, as if his entire family had gone away. Noah's absence made her feel terribly lonely. She hadn't acknowledged how comforting it was to know that he was always there, watching out for her, across the street. Poor Noah, she thought, feeling guilty that she'd doubted him. Whatever had happened must have been awful. She texted him again: *R u OK? Rly worried about you xxx.*

No reply came, so she opened the front door and walked into the hall, catching sight of herself in the mirror. The zits on her chin were glowing angrily again. She took off her coat, went upstairs and put her bag down on her bed, taking out the stolen cardigan and folding it into a neat square, so that, for now, the incriminating tag was out of view. Then she switched on her computer. She intended to check her Facebook account, and she thought she might send Noah a quick email too, just in case he couldn't text her. She opened up her email programme, expecting to find the usual junk that collected there while she was out at school. What she didn't expect to see was a message with the heading: *Important. Please Read.* The sender was named Robyn Hood.

Chapter 23

From: Robyn Hood
Subject: Important. Please read.
Date: 20th April 6:00 PM
To: Ruby Collins

Hi Ruby,

If you haven't already guessed, it's Noah here.

Before I start, I want to say sorry. I'm sorry I've stolen your name and I'm sorry for what I'm about to do. I know you'll be angry with me and that you might even hate me, but one day you'll understand why I've done it. One day you'll realise I did it for you.

If you're thinking of rushing around to my house, don't! It's too late to stop me and I won't be at home, anyway. I wrote this email hours ago, but I delayed it, to make sure you didn't receive it until you got back from school. I couldn't risk you trying to talk me out of this. I don't know exactly where I'll be when you read this. At the police station, probably. That's where I'm going as soon as I've finished typing this email.

As you must have guessed by now, I'm going to tell the police that I am Robyn Hood. And they are going to believe me because I've got all the evidence to prove it. Once they see it, they won't care that I'm a guy and Robyn Hood is supposed to be a girl. Like you said, you can be whoever you want to be in a blog. I'm not going to get technical on you, but I can show them the computer codes, the traces from when I set up the blog and from every time I moved it for you. If that's not enough, I can also give them physical evidence: the earrings you took. The shop will have reported them stolen, and they've got a serial number on them (which I don't think you noticed). I'm sorry I lied and said I'd thrown them away.

But I don't think the police will be very interested in Robyn Hood, a blog and a bit of shoplifting when they find out what else I've been up to. Remember when you got caught at Zenda and I rescued you by pretending to be your dad? You asked how I paid for the tops you stole and I told you not to worry about it. It was better that you didn't know. I actually paid for them using your dad's credit card. It was a stupid thing to do, but I had to think fast, and I had access to the details right in front of me. What I didn't tell you is that my hacking programme has given me access to the bank account and credit card details of everyone we know. I could have spent millions, if I'd wanted to, but I only ever meant to show up the gaps in the system. Still, I couldn't not help you when you needed it. I can't believe your dad never said anything about it, that he didn't notice he'd spent money at a shop called Zenda, when he couldn't have been there. Please say sorry to him from me.

I don't know what will happen to me now. Internet credit card fraud is pretty serious. Maybe they'll let me off with a warning, or maybe they'll throw the book at me and cart me off to a young offenders' institution. Only joking. Hey, I might even get offered a job at Microsoft or in the Secret Service, hacking into terrorist websites. Don't worry about me, OK? I was going to tell the police about the hacking soon, anyway. They need to know because if I can hack into those sites, so can other people – serious criminals. This way, I've killed two birds with one stone and saved you doing something you'd regret. Whatever you say, Ruby, you don't always want to be known as the girl who was Robyn Hood. You don't want to be remembered for being a shoplifter, a thief. You're worth so much more than that, if only you could see it.

I guess you'll probably never talk to me again now, will you? If I thought there was a way to avoid losing you, I wouldn't do this. But I can't see one. I know that you'll never think I'm good enough for you. I know that whatever you say you'll never be able to tell your friends about us. And I know that the blog has been tying us together. So, whatever happens, I'm sure I'm going to lose you. At least, by doing this, I get to save you first.

Be happy, Ruby. Please don't hate me.

Love Noah x

Ruby read Noah's email five times, in the vain hope that on the next reading, or the one after that, it might say something different. But, however many times she scanned them, the words didn't change, and neither did their meaning. Noah had taken matters into his own hands and it was too late for her to do anything about it. He had helped her create Robyn Hood and now he'd taken her away. It wasn't fair. It just wasn't fair! And yet . . . it was amazing too, that he cared about her that much, that he'd sacrificed himself for her. For *her*. How many times had he saved her now – three, four? An image of his lovely face came into her mind and she felt a surge of warmth in her belly. God, she wanted to talk to him now. He was incredible and she really didn't deserve him, not after the way she'd treated him. But wasn't he stupid! And why hadn't he talked to her first? And it wasn't really his decision to make, was it?

She was so full of conflicting, tangled-up feelings that didn't know what to do. This sticky mess of emotion clung to her insides like treacle. If she tried to vocalise it she knew it would only come out, wordless, in an ear-splitting scream. Instead, she spun about her room like a demented insect, until she'd burned up so much energy that she collapsed on her bed and lay there breathing hard for several minutes. Then, in a panic, she printed out Noah's email twice. After all, if he was able to delay its arrival with his technical wizardry, who was to say that he wasn't also able to make it self-destruct after she'd read it?

When she'd calmed down a little she began to think more rationally. All day, people had been saying that Robyn Hood had handed *herself* in; they must, unknowingly, have been talking about Noah. Who else knew the truth? Was it on the internet already? Had it been there all day? Why hadn't she persisted in finding out? She sat down at her computer and did another search. The story was everywhere now, all over the web.

The mystery of the identity of the shoplifting blogger known as Robyn Hood appears finally to have been solved. This morning, a youth handed himself into London police, voluntarily. He is believed to be a teenage boy, not a girl as previously suspected. He is also helping the police with other matters relating to credit card fraud and internet security. It's unknown whether his name will be released.

So Noah's name wasn't out there yet. Was it just a matter of time, or could she still do something to stop it? Like her, he was still only fifteen. Sometimes the media wasn't allowed to reveal your name if you weren't an adult. Maybe it would all still be OK. She had Noah's email, and it proved that she was the guilty one, that he was just covering for her. Noah hadn't thought of that when he sent it, had he? Maybe she could go to the police station right now, with the email and the stolen cardigan and hand herself in too. If she talked to her dad, she could get him to say he'd agreed to pay for the tops, and then Noah wouldn't have done anything wrong at all. Noah didn't deserve to be punished when her dad hadn't even noticed the money was missing. How could he not have questioned spending all that money in a woman's clothes shop? Didn't he look at his credit card statements?

Her thoughts were interrupted by the appearance of an instant message on her computer screen. It was Amanda.

– *Oh my God, Ruby! Have you heard about Noah Baker? Turns out he's Robyn Hood!*

So, it was already too late. If Amanda knew, Noah's name must have got out. Ruby felt a rush of nausea.

– *Who told you that?*

– *Everyone's talking about it at school. One of the lads has a brother who's a policeman and he let it slip. Best gossip ever! I'd never have guessed it in a million years. What a freak! Pretending to be a girl – you couldn't make it up. He's seriously twisted.*

Ruby imagined what it would be like at school the next day, when the news had spread. Hideous. Whatever happened, Noah would never be able to go back there. He'd ruined his life for her. And she hadn't even had the guts to tell her friends she was seeing him. She was hurt that Amanda had called him a freak. That was what everyone would be thinking now, wasn't it? Noah wasn't a freak, he was an amazing person, a better friend to her than Amanda would ever be.

– *Leave him alone*, she typed, and logged off. She wasn't angry with Noah any more, she was furious with Amanda and, most of all, with herself. She lay down on her bed and waited for the inevitable phone call. Amanda and Hanni were just like Tweedledum and Tweedledee. Amanda would have rung Hanni the second she realised Ruby was upset, and they'd be discussing her right now. Hanni would be reassuring Amanda that she'd done nothing wrong, and then she'd volunteer to call Ruby to find out what was going on. I give her five minutes, Ruby thought, maybe ten.

'Ruby, what's going on?' asked Hanni, after just seven minutes. 'I've spoken to Mand and she said you were all funny with her and then you went offline. She told me about Noah, obviously. That must have been a shock! God, he really is a weird stalker after all! And he's been living across the road from you all this time. You're lucky he didn't do anything to you! Oh my God, I've just remembered he came into your bedroom when I was in there. Eugh! Creepy!'

'Don't you dare say anything bad about him,' Ruby warned Hanni. She felt so furious that she was trembling. 'Or I'll put the phone down right now.'

'Jesus, Ruby, what's got into you? Your voice sounds so mean it's scary.'

'I don't like people saying nasty stuff about Noah, that's what.'

'I know he was your friend and all when you were a kid, but he's turned out to be a complete psycho. You should be pleased you found out the truth. Why are you worried what people think of him?'

'Why do you think? Because I like him. He's my friend. If I turned out to be Robyn Hood, would you stop talking to me? Would you think I was a freak and a weirdo?'

'No, course not. But that's ridiculous, anyway. It wouldn't happen.'

Just you wait and see, thought Ruby. 'Well, neither is he.'

Hanni paused. 'Oh my God, Rubes,' she said, her tone incredulous. 'It's all starting to make sense now. You really do like him, don't you?'

'Yes,' said Ruby, finding courage from somewhere. 'I *really* like him.' The words she'd been holding back for weeks, barely acknowledging herself, began to spill out of her. She felt light-headed and breathless, her voice shaky. 'And the truth is I've been seeing Noah for months.' Now her honesty had its own momentum; she couldn't stop. 'And you know what? I think he's amazing. Not a nerd or a geek, but gorgeous and kind and clever. He's way better than me, or any of us.'

Hanni was struck silent, an event which occurred so rarely that, in different circumstances, Ruby would have savoured it. 'You're having a laugh,' she said eventually, but it was clear from her voice that she didn't believe her own words. 'You're taking the piss.'

'No,' said Ruby. 'No, I'm not. It's the truth. I swear on my life. I've been wanting to tell you for ages but I saw what you all thought about him, and I couldn't. Well, now you know.'

She hung up the phone before Hanni could reply, her hands shaking so much that she struggled to find the button. She couldn't quite believe what she'd just done – it was either the best or the craziest speech she'd ever made. Had she just wrecked her closest friendships? She was so exhilarated, so high on adrenalin that, in that moment, she felt it didn't matter. If her friends truly cared about her, they'd understand. If they didn't, then they weren't worth her friendship, were they?

There was no time to worry about it now. She had important things to do, and her mum would be home from work very soon. She looked at her watch. If she was going to go, she had about half an hour to prepare herself.

She changed out of her school uniform into her most flattering jeans and her favourite green jumper, brushed her hair and put on some make-up, covering up her zits as best she could. Then she put the stolen cardigan into a plastic bag, together with a copy of Noah's email, and she scribbled a short note, explaining and apologising to her parents. She left them all on the kitchen table. She wasn't sure when she'd be back, or if she'd have a chance to call.

There were hordes of people waiting outside the police station, many of them holding cameras and notebooks. They looked cold and frustrated, as if they'd been standing around for hours. Ruby pushed past them, through the entrance doors and into the waiting room. She felt nervous now, wobbly, unsure whether she was doing the right thing.

'Can I help you?' asked the officer at the front desk. He seemed too old and too fat to be a policeman.

'I'm just waiting for someone,' she said. 'For Noah Baker.'

'I see,' he said, peering at her quizzically. She clearly wasn't a journalist. 'You should really be outside. Your name?'

'It's Robyn,' she said. 'Are you going to let Noah out soon? Are you charging him with anything?'

'I can't give out that type of information, I'm afraid. Now, if you don't mind waiting outside with the others.'

'OK,' she said. She took a deep breath. 'But I've got some evidence, it might be important.' She reached into her jacket pocket and took out a piece of paper, unfolding it, and smoothing out the creases. 'Here.'

'Leave it on here and I'll make sure the right person gets it,' said the policeman. 'Robyn, did you say?' He raised his eyebrows.

'Yeah, that's right,' she said. 'Robyn, with a "y".' She left Noah's email, still folded, on the desk. 'Please can you tell Noah I'm here. I'll be waiting outside if you need me . . .'

She turned and walked slowly to the exit. The throng was still outside, the journalists and photographers jostling each other to catch sight of whoever was coming out. A few hopeful flashes went off, then died away. Self-consciously, Ruby made her way back into the pack and waited. She didn't know what else to do. Minutes passed, or maybe hours; she'd lost all sense of time. At last, the doors opened and she watched as Noah walked outside, his parents a few paces behind him. He looked sullen but unashamed, and so grown-up, so handsome. Ruby felt a rush of pride. He's mine, she thought, everyone wants him now, but he cares about *me*. Then the crowd surged behind her and swallowed her up.

'Noah!' she cried, raising her arms, helplessly. She couldn't see through the blur of bodies and flashes. 'I'm over here!'

He didn't hear her, or if he did, he didn't respond.

'Do you know him?' asked the reporter standing next to her.

'Oh yes,' said Ruby, smiling up at her. 'He's my boyfriend.'

'Interesting.' The reporter's pen was poised above her notepad. 'Tell me more . . .' she said.

Chapter 24

Ruby watched out for Noah through a crack in the living room curtains. If she craned her neck she could just see up to his bedroom window. She had been watching for hours, waiting and hoping to see him, but he hadn't appeared. She'd caught glimpses of other faces, unfamiliar, serious-looking men, who must had been dismantling his computer equipment, because a little later she'd seen the same men carrying out boxes to a black car and driving away. She guessed they were police, gathering evidence to take back to the station. Strange people had been going in and out of Noah's house all evening. Now it was dark and the visitors had stopped coming. It was funny that she had never noticed before how quiet her street was. It made her feel even more alone.

Her mum had found the package and called her dad,

just as she'd expected. They had been waiting to ambush her in the hall when she got home from the police station. Mum looked as if she'd been crying a lot, which made Ruby feel guilty. She wondered if her dad had comforted her, or if he'd looked away in embarrassment, like he usually did. They hadn't shouted much this time; it had all been said before. Ruby was just relieved that finally they accepted her story. Her dad had gone home now. Tomorrow morning, they would all go down to the police station together. By then, the newspaper would be out. And what would happen to her after that was anybody's guess.

For now, she had been grounded for a month, her mobile phone confiscated and her own computer removed from her bedroom, which meant she couldn't even chat to her friends. Not that she was sure they would be talking to her any more, anyway. It struck her that she didn't care much. All that mattered was what Noah thought. All that mattered was that he still wanted her. There was so much she needed to say to him, and so much lost time to make up for. Her longing for him was almost like a physical pain, bursting out of her, stretching her bones and her skin. They could send her to jail, make her do community work, take away all her things; as long as she hadn't lost Noah.

At about ten o' clock, she heard the sound of a car pulling up outside and she felt a surge of adrenalin in her chest. Through the gap in the curtains she could just

213

make out Noah, silhouetted against the back window of his dad's estate car. He was sitting absolutely still. She watched as his parents got out of the front doors, slamming them shut, and his dad walked around to the back to open the door for Noah, as if he were a young child again. Noah seemed to hesitate for a moment before climbing out. Ruby wanted to shout to him, to run out of her house to greet him, but she knew she couldn't. Instead, she opened the curtains wider and pressed her face up against the window. Please turn around, she prayed silently, please turn around.

Ruby stared at Noah's back as he followed his parents along the short path to his house. When they reached the front door, the security light came on, and she could see him clearly: tall and slender and gorgeous. His parents disappeared inside, leaving him alone for a moment on the doorstep. And then, just as Ruby was about to give up hope, he turned around and looked directly at her. He held her gaze for a few seconds, so intensely that it took away her breath, and then he smiled and nodded, before slowly turning away and closing the front door behind him.

Acknowledgements

Big thanks to Stephanie Thwaites at Curtis Brown,
and to the team at Piccadilly Press: Brenda Gardner,
Anne Clark, Melissa Hyder, Margot Edwards,
Vivien Tesseras, Geoff Barlow, Lea Garton,
Simon Davis and Geoffrey Lill.
Eternal love and gratitude to all my fabulous friends
and family, especially to Steve, Mum and Dad,
and Judy. Thanks to the Owl Bookshop,
Kentish Town for putting on superb launches.
Cheers to Rick Bronks of Satureyes, for his services
as a photographer (and his software). Thank you to
Dr Jessica Baron for fixing me up and to
Professor Robert Reiner for the criminology lesson.
And finally, *merci beaucoup* to all my friends at the
Citea Nice Magnan, without whose hospitality this
book would still not be finished: David, Marlene,
Aurelie, Julie, Sylvain, Remi, Farid, Najar Karim and
Super Mario. (See, I told you I would!)

Loving DANNY

HILARY FREEMAN

Naomi is restless. She's on her gap year and stuck at home with her parents while all her friends are travelling or away at university. Then she meets Danny, a mysterious and intense musician who opens her eyes to a whole new world around her.

Danny is exciting and talented, and his band are on the brink of stardom. But he also has a dark, destructive side . . . Will Naomi be able to save Danny before it's too late? And, more importantly, can she save herself?

'The perfect choice for teenage girls. Warm and witty, compelling and insightful, it's a great read.'
Sunday Express

HILARY FREEMAN

Lily believes her boyfriend Jack is perfect, but
wonders why he won't talk about his past.
Wouldn't it be fantastic, she thinks, if she could talk
to his ex and fill in all the gaps?

Lily devises a way to do just that.
But what begins as a bit of fun has unexpected –
and disturbing – consequences . . .

Don't Ask is a story about love, friendship and secrets.
Sometimes it's better not to ask too many questions.

'Completely riveting from start to finish.
Thoroughly recommended!' *Chicklish*

'The characters are believable and the narrative is
pacy . . . a good read.' *School Librarian*

www.piccadillypress.co.uk

☆ The latest news on forthcoming books

☆ Chapter previews

☆ Author biographies

☆ Fun quizzes

☆ Reader reviews

☆ Competitions and fab prizes

☆ Book features and cool downloads

☆ And much, much more . . .

Log on and check it out!

Piccadilly Press